Mad About The Baron

MAD ABOUT
THE BARON

Bianca Blythe

Contents

Chapter One

G rooms were not supposed to abandon their brides at altars, and nobody seemed less inclined to act ungallantly than the wondrous, utterly splendid, Lord Bertrand Braunschweig, Baron of Wolbert.

Veronique Daventry, stepsister to the Duke of Alfriston, checked again that her train fanned dramatically behind her. The silk thread embroidered on the dress sparkled under the candlelight.

Perfect.

The vicar cleared his throat in a somber manner. "Are you certain the groom is arriving, lassie?"

"He'll be here," Veronique said.

One didn't write a woman that one intended to marry her and then not bother to make an appearance at the chapel.

The vicar did not display the appropriate degree of confidence at the words, despite the frequency of Veronique's assertions.

Never mind.

A lack of timeliness was not the worst quality in a man.

What were mere minutes compared to an eternity of love? Her momentary discomfit at the vicar's scrutiny would be more than worth it for the lifelong delight the baron would experience at glimpsing her for the first time.

Veronique had corresponded with Lord Braunschweig for two years, ever since he'd asked Mr. Simons for an introduction. No pleasure exceeded that of receiving a letter from him. She'd long memorized the exact sweep of his quill, the calligraphy often imperfect, as if he'd not been able to control his eagerness as he wrote her.

The wind swept through the cracked stained glass windows, and the vicar placed a blanket over his legs.

Veronique's neck was cold. As were her arms. The problem with sheer, shimmering gowns that clung to one's body in an alluring fashion were that they were in no way designed for the frigid Scottish temperature.

Catholics had been correct to insist on high collars and strategically placed vestments. Perhaps Veronique should have researched the elopement policies in France or Italy rather than Scotland.

No matter.

Maybe the man was lost. He was Austrian. He could be forgiven for being befuddled by the novel landscape of the Highlands. The poor baron must be beside himself with agony.

The vicar coughed, the noise amplified by the chapel's acoustics. "When you wrote me to say you desired a wedding, I imagined you'd be bringing more people to witness the event than your maid."

"She is a good maid."

"Most women bring their family to such occasions, lassie. Surely you must be in possession of a single acquaintance?"

She thought of her family, settled in Lord Rockport's parlor, blissfully unaware she was marrying a few yards away. Likely they were sipping tea and debating the merits of haggis.

She wanted her first meeting with her future husband to be alone, and not in the presence of her loud-mouthed relations. "Their company is not required."

The vicar scrutinized her. "Your accent is foreign."

She shivered, but steeled her features. She refused to succumb to the faint doubt that threatened to appear whenever people examined her skin tone too closely, no matter how smugly their lips turned up when they decided they had an advantage over her.

She would not allow this man, charged with ministering a small population in a remote mountainous village, to think himself superior to her. Tens of thousands of women adored her work.

"Your letters arrived from the former colonies," the vicar continued, but it was more of a question than a statement, and she turned away.

The outline of Diomhair Caisteal, a grandiose compilation of steep walls and narrow turrets, loomed through the few window panes not graced with stained glass. Her stepsister, Louisa, had recently wed Lady Rockport's brother, and her stepmother had become so overcome with emotion, that she'd succumbed to Veronique's pleas to accompany her family to the British Isles.

She smiled. They'd be so delighted when she presented her new husband to them.

Her stepmother frequently lamented the challenge of finding Veronique a fiancé, and she'd long dreamed of surprising them with a husband. Her skin tone might be unconventional, but that wouldn't stop her from romance.

The vicar continued to direct a disapproving look in her direction, but she refused to yield to any unfounded misgivings he might have.

Veronique addressed her maid. "Please search for the baron in the village."

"Very well, miss." The girl dipped into a curtsy.

"Tell him to hurry." Veronique glanced again at the vicar who stood near the candelabras, as if hopeful for warmth.

"The chapel is on a hill," the vicar said sternly. "It would be highly unlikely for the man to miss it. If he were to overlook so commanding and elegant a structure as this chapel, it might signify greater troubles in your marriage."

Veronique frowned. Her stepbrother was a duke, she was engaged to a baron, but more than that, she was wealthy and esteemed. Most people had heard of her, even if they were unfamiliar with her Christian name, and she summoned her most regal mannerism. "Is patience no longer a virtue to be lauded?"

"Well—" The man's face reddened, perhaps aided by a habit of sipping whisky and wine.

She shrugged.

The baron would arrive.

He needs to.

Chapter Two

Nothing in the world surpassed a carriage ride through the Scottish Highlands in utter intolerability. The constant, unpredictable swerve of the mail coach, coupled with the distinct lessening of interior standards compared to its English counterparts, rendered the experience insufferable.

Miles thanked his ancestors for having the foresight to plant an estate in a more sensible region: Kent. The county's green hills never ventured into mountainous territory.

Unfortunately Miles's half-brother's ancestral line had shown considerable less foresight, which had led to Miles's current predicament. He strove to counteract the crisis by the most efficient means possible: feigning sleep.

If he shut his eyes long enough, perhaps actual sleep would occur, even if the other travelers seemed intent on hampering that possibility, exclaiming with an overabundance of enthusiasm over every view composed of goats grasping onto soggy slopes with their hoofs.

The passengers equaled him in Englishness—clearly

Scotsmen possessed too much sense to venture into one of these horrid contraptions.

If only he could ride his favorite horse here, yet he refused to submit Hercules to a long journey only to end in the icy gales and incessant sludge of the Highlands.

"Do you think that's him?" A high-pitched voice squeaked with the vigor of a violin in the hands of a tone-deaf abecedarian.

Normally the shrill pitch might have discomfited him, though his mind was thoroughly occupied with her words.

"Whom do you mean?" a second soprano voice asked.

"Why Lord Worthing, naturally!"

Blast.

He resisted the urge to open his eyes. Or frown.

It had happened. They'd discovered him.

He'd thought he might be secure in Scotland. The war had ended two years ago, and he'd hoped people might have forgotten the depictions of him in heroic situations across the continent.

"It can't be him. I always supposed Lord Worthing to be tall."

Blood surged through Miles's veins.

"Now ladies," a third female voice, gruffer and riddled with a sarcasm indicating a woman in belief of a possession of intelligence said, "He is sitting."

Perhaps this was their long-suffering mother. Or virginal great aunt.

"He is handsome," one of the women across him mused.

Miles did not permit himself to smile. The chit had called him short. Forgiveness was not a state to be entered lightly.

"Though I did imagine his hair to be nicer," she continued.

Some statements were intolerable.

Miles clenched his fingers, inhaled, and opened his eyes.

There were three of them: a plain-faced woman beside him, the severity of her face not lessened by her tightly pulled back knot, and two other women opposite him, attired in bright Scottish tartan. The garish fabric was the sort no actual Scotswomen would parade about in, but which some women in possession of an abundance of money, not bestowed with a similar abundance of sense, allowed their dressmakers to persuade them to buy.

"I am indeed Lord Worthing," he declared, appreciating how their eyes widened and took on a familiar dewy expression that tended to occur right before certain chits dropped their handkerchiefs.

"How exciting," the woman beside him said, creasing her gray dress as she leaned closer.

Definitely not a married woman. No man would tie himself to a creature so lacking in fashion sense.

Likely she was a governess, or a poor relative tasked to be the companion to children with whom the parents could not fathom conversing.

"It is most unfair to judge my hair when it is pouring outside." He firmed his demeanor, summoning the aristocratic outrage his ancestors must have faced when confronted with the Normans' invasion. "Even Brummel himself couldn't help but have his coiffure look inelegantly tousled."

The chits should have looked ashamed: that was the natural reaction to being chastised.

Instead they beamed, the fact highlighted by their generous application of vermilion. "It's truly you."

"Naturally."

"Thank you, heavens," the chit opposite him shouted, flinging her nondescript brown curls to the side. Her sister, judging from the similar hair shade, refrained from speaking, though she did clap.

Loudly.

He eyed them warily. This was no time for joy.

He drew himself up, emphasizing the length of his torso when he was not occupied with attempting sleep, and directed his loftiest stare at them. "No one could feign my appearance."

They had the audacity to giggle, and Miles scowled.

"We were thinking you might be here," the first chit confided.

"Why ever would you think that?" Horror surged through him. This was Scotland. Not a battlefield. Not a war tattered town. Not even Mayfair.

He didn't desire to get the reputation of a man who frequented this dismal land. There was no war for him to report on, only brownish grassland gorged with goats.

And perhaps one anonymous authoress.

"Your half-brother lives near here. Lord Rockport," she added, as if he might have forgotten the name.

Miles crossed his arms.

"We were hopeful you might be visiting," she continued, "and here you are."

"How nice for you," he said.

"Yes," the woman across from him assented. "We've been in Scotland for months, but this will make everyone most jealous."

"An emotion important to spread." He waited for their

faces to pale, but they blinked up at him, their faces still adorned with unwavering smiles.

"You are one of my charges' favorite celebrities," the woman beside him confided. "They've expressed admiration for the chiseled features of your face."

Miles relaxed slightly.

His features *were* impeccable.

Maintaining a stony expression was more challenging than he'd assumed. He wondered at his tutors' ability to emanate arrogance with unflappable consistency. Though then again, likely they had never been subjected to such blatant flattery.

Still, he could not reward the women with conversation for being in possession of eyesight, and he refrained from gracing them with a smile.

They still hadn't mentioned his actual accomplishments, ones that surpassed even his ability to maintain a modicum of suavity.

There'd once been a time when he'd traveled around Europe, evading cavalry charges and blue-garbed Frenchmen brandishing muskets. That had been a bloody good time.

He hadn't fought, but he'd done something better: he'd reported the news to the world.

Now there was no war. Bonaparte had capitulated, and Miles was back in Britain. His editor had assigned him to find a woman calling herself Loretta Van Lochen.

It was a hard fall.

Such frivolities held no interest to him. Unfortunately her undeniable fame interested his publisher, who desired to expand the newspapers female readership.

If only the English government possessed less skill at

diplomacy, and he might visit a region which was not habituated mainly by livestock.

Miles was famous for reporting in the midst of danger, but not for writing about...novelists.

Particularly of penny dreadfuls.

"Since we are acquainted with your name," the woman beside him said, interrupting him from his gloomy musings, "I must take it upon myself to introduce myself—and my charges—to you."

Miles frowned. He favored resuming an attempt at sleep.

"I am *Miss* Hesper Haskett." She lingered on her salutation, emphasizing her unmarried status, as if urging him to change it.

"I see," Miles replied icily.

Etiquette might dictate that he should express some pleasure at meeting her, but he'd never been one for propriety, especially for people who questioned his attractiveness.

"These are my charges: Miss Theodosia Fitzroy and Miss Amaryllis Fitzroy."

"Our parents didn't want us to travel in the same carriage as them," Miss Amaryllis Fitzroy said gaily. "Apparently we are quite talkative!"

Miles composed his face into the sort of stern expression his father had never possessed, choosing instead to channel the austere gaze of his instructors.

There had to be some advantages to attending Eton beyond the memorization of Virgil.

Miss Haskett continued to stare at him, and unease trickled through Miles. Did Miss Haskett's scrutiny need to be so unwavering? Miles was certain there had once been greater space between them, not that the coach could be described as expansive. Perhaps the Scottish owners had desired to economize, or perhaps the Scottish were narrower-hipped than their English counterparts, owing to the prevalence of inedible dishes such as haggis and black pudding.

Miss Haskett's charges still seemed affected by his presence, judging from their glazed eyes.

Miles directed his vision downward.

Perhaps pushing his arms against his chest emphasized the broadness of said chest or the muscular form of his arms. Indeed, some women might even find his stony expression appealing, bequeathing him with mystery.

"The coach driver informed us there will be another stop before we reach the coast." Miss Haskett gazed meaningfully at him. "Wouldn't it be pleasant to partake in some repast at the posting inn?"

"Well..." Miles was hungry—not that he would confide that to Miss Haskett.

"We can all dine together!" Miss Theodora Fitzroy clapped her hands.

"Lord Worthing is a baron," Miss Haskett replied. "He is a man of much importance and may be reluctant to dine with ladies who have not even debuted yet."

"Oh," the chits' gleeful expressions rearranged themselves to something resembling devastation.

"Though perhaps..." Miss Haskett leaned nearer him, and a thick floral scent invaded his nostrils. There could be no earthly reason for the scent of roses to be quite so potent in this tiny carriage, all the way in the Highlands in the middle of January. She tossed her head. "The baron likely favors dining with me."

"As a matter of fact—" Miles doubted the propriety of

having the gap between them be so thoroughly narrowed and edged nearer the window.

"You can regale me with stories of your adventures."

"Well..." He strove to find an excuse to dine alone.

"Do you not adore posting inns?" Miss Haskett remarked. "Especially in this region. They are always so...empty."

Miles firmed his expression. Thank goodness for gloves. No need for anyone to see blood rushing to his wrists before he clenched them.

He knew what this woman desired.

She wanted him to take her to such a room—and then be discovered by her charges.

He scowled. He refused to be compromised. That was something that happened to other aristocrats.

He was a former war correspondent. Perhaps now there was no use for him to work abroad, but one day there would be.

The chits chattered on, and eventually the coach slowed and pulled into the posting inn.

"Finally!" The ladies scuttled down the steep screeching steps of the carriage, swishing their pelisses over his boots, their faces still grinning, as if they desired to tell everyone that they'd come close to touching.

Miss Haskett extended a gloved hand in his direction, and Miles's stomach constricted as her fingers tightened around his.

He helped her to her feet, and her eyelashes batted with a rapidity warranted for confronting a dust storm.

"Thank you, Lord Worthing."

"Er—yes." He scrambled from the carriage, and his spine stiffened as the carriage steps squeaked behind him.

"Shall we...dine?" Miss Haskett's voice seemed to have

dropped an octave. Ever since a certain *Matchmaking for Wallflowers* article, all the ladies had taken to lowering their voices in an effort at seduction.

Miles did not want to be seduced.

Not now. Not ever.

He was cold and wet and hungry.

The Scottish gales swirled with an unrelenting gusto, as if desiring praise for their blustering puissance. Patches of snow melted over the soggy mud, and the posting inn, hunched over a steep slope, scarcely inspired confidence.

Miles trudged toward the half-timbered structure, noting how the thatched roof sagged under some not yet melting snow. Hopefully they'd managed to learn how to pour ale into a tankard and make a decent meat pie. The inn looked like it had had sufficient centuries to practice.

Miss Haskett entered the inn before him, joining her charges. His nose pinched in the cold, and a cloud of gray smoke spurted with every breath, perhaps to assure him he'd not frozen yet.

They disappeared around a corner after ordering, and Miles approached the barmaid. Her lips seemed to curl.

"This way, sir. There's a fire in the room. You'll be warm in no time." The words seemed to make her eyes sparkle. Clearly Scots had very little to amuse themselves, or perhaps she'd simply never seen a person so clearly in need of warmth before.

He frowned. Perhaps he hadn't needed to arrive at Gerard's in a tweed coat, even though his tailor had insisted it was the very latest in fashion.

Perhaps he might even have selected a cravat fabric that better protected his neck against the cold. But still. Surely that alone shouldn't be cause for merriment. Was the woman able to tell from his mere stride that he did not belong in this vile country?

He sighed.

Perhaps.

After all he was very English.

His ancestors may have settled in Kent, but they'd made the move from Sussex. His ancestors had married some Norman aristocrats, ones who, when not occupying themselves with invading, used a modicum of manners learned from their time on the continent.

"Shouldn't I order?"

She laughed. "There's only one meal 'ere, Lord Worthing."

Evidently Scotland received broadsheets too. He'd been a bloody good correspondent.

"This way," she said briskly. "I know just where to seat you."

He followed her past some tables, noting the driver mingling with some locals.

The barmaid's gait did not waver, and she opened a door

He ducked under the low wooden beam and took a seat. "I'll bring you yer grub now."

"Thank you—"

The door clicked behind him as she exited, and he frowned. And then shrugged.

Some people were taken aback to be so near to the presence of a person so important. Miles had never been asked for directions so much since becoming famous, and he was accustomed to young women approaching and giggling as they inquired about the location of Westminster Abbey or St. Paul's Cathedral, when any fool could spot the spires soaring above the other city buildings.

He glanced around the dimly lit room. He had the strange sensation that he was being observed, even though the barmaid had just left.

"We are alone," a feminine voice sounded behind him, and his heart sank.

He turned around and braced himself.

*

Miss Haskett stood before him.

His eyebrows rose. He'd always assumed governesses to value rules, given their proclivity to occupy the greater portion of their time in trying to impart order to others.

"I told my charges to give us privacy." Miss Haskett flung her hair, and her straight locks tumbled inelegantly downward. She strode toward him, and for a horrible second he wondered whether she might plop herself on his lap to better be available for admiration.

The woman seemed to have found time to change: she'd replaced her somber gray frock for a slightly more vivacious dark blue. Two rows of pearls dangled from her neck. The jewels were of such a grandiose size that he wondered if she'd taken the necklace from one of her charges.

A gasp seemed to sound inside the room.

He scrutinized the shadowed sections of the room, the places that the single tallow candle did not reach. Was it possible someone was hiding behind one of the centuries-old pillars?

"Baron," Miss Haskett said quickly.

"You shouldn't be here," Miles said.

"How pleasant to find you worry about me."

He swallowed hard. "If anyone found you here—"

Marriage.

That was the sort of thing that might happen.

He'd had sufficient chits place themselves in his paths and start undressing. They tended to have scheming mamas or financially desperate papas.

He knew friends who'd been felled by these manipulations. His old friend Toppy was never at his London club, tasked with producing sufficient heirs and spares to give his new wife, whom he'd found undressed behind a balcony curtain shortly before her loud-mouth mama happened upon them.

Lord Markham, a man who'd never expressed much interest in women and had a rumored preference for certain Soho molly houses, had been caught with a woman in a maze at a house party. Lord Markham did not seem to be the type to succumb to such passions, and the poor man must be miserable ensconced with his new wife and parents-in-law in a dilapidating manor house in Cornwall.

Lord Worthing directed his attention to Miss Haskett. "Please leave."

Uncertainty flickered over her face, but she inhaled. "And waste this opportunity?"

She seemed to be striving to lower a capped sleeve down her shoulder, and she frowned as her hands yanked the fabric.

"In truth," Lord Worthing said, forcing his tone to sound apologetic and gentlemanly, "I just want to eat."

"Me?" Her face flushed, but she managed to retain eye contact with him. He had to admire her for that.

And then he heard something that sounded like shuffling.

Something that sounded *very* much like shuffling.

Blast.

He had to leave. At any moment somebody might pop from behind a column. He sprinted from the door.

"I see you," a high-pitched voice, perhaps Amaryllis, shouted behind him, but she was too late. He would not allow anyone to compromise him.

He enjoyed his life.

He enjoyed his bachelor ways, and refused to be saddled with a wife, no matter her cleverness at concocting compromising situations.

He rushed through the pub and grabbed a piece of bread some guest had left behind.

"Don't bother with the meal," he gasped to the barmaid as he gobbled the too stale roll.

He pushed open the door and rushed over the damp grass and patches of snow toward the coach.

A groom was supervising the switching of horses.

"Will be a while before you can go," the man said.

"I want to ride the rest of the way myself."

The coach driver narrowed his eyes. "On these roads?"

"What are a few holes?" Miles attempted to smile brightly.

He was a good rider. He would certainly be able to do anything that a Scottish farmer had to do on occasion.

Even if the drizzle didn't seem exactly pleasant, and even if the heaps of melting snow and sludge did not seem enticing.

"I rather fancy the quiet," Miles said.

"Aye." The coach driver nodded. "You'll find that 'ere. Reckon you can't find much quiet in London with all those society parties." He winked. "Don't think I don't recognize you."

"Does everyone?" Miles asked faintly.

Normally he would be proud of his carefully cultivated reputation, but now the path to his brother's castle seemed of the unpleasant variety.

"One moment." The coachman scrambled to his seat and found a spare sheet of paper amongst more official looking documents and maps. He picked up a quill and quickly dipped it into ink, so it dripped onto the paper. "Care to make an autograph? For my...son?"

"Naturally." Miles asked him his son's name and addressed it.

The door to the public house swung open, and Miss Haskett stepped outside. She strode directly toward him, her two charges in tow.

Miles scribbled his signature hastily. "I really must go." He took one of the horses that was being lined up. "How much to borrow this one?"

"But that's something you should arrange with the groomsman 'ere," the coach driver shouted.

"No time," Miles said hastily and threw some notes at the coachman. "You arrange it!"

The man glanced at the money. "But that's more than enough to buy the horse."

Miles grinned. "Good."

He swung onto the startled horse and urged it to a gallop. It was unfortunate he hadn't had time to have a proper saddle put on the horse, but it didn't matter. Miles excelled at horse riding, even if riding through Scotland on the type of frigid day that should be devoted purely to hot chocolate drinking was suboptimal.

He inhaled the crisp air and guided the horse through the smattering of thatched-roofed homes that made up the village.

The horse's hooves clopped a happy rhythm over the path, and Miles guided it in the direction of the castle.

Soon he would see his family, but now he could enjoy freedom from the carriage and its occupants, even if the rain had turned into the freezing variety.

Miles urged his horse forward, and it galloped over the ever-rockier terrain. Rain drops scattered over him, obscuring the tall brown slopes the Scots tended to extol.

Chapter Three

The rain increased, and Miles almost regretted his athletic urge to arrive on horseback. Coaches had their advantages, even if they did have a propensity to be filled with the more scheming of the other sex.

Blast.

He'd rather expected to appear in more style than sweeping his muddied boots and water-soaked cloak about Gerard's castle.

Rain tumbled down on him as he neared Diomhair Caisteal, and Miles sympathized with the sour expressions that graced his Scottish counterparts with the regularity of smiles on the English.

One likely wouldn't take an optimistic outlook on the world after tramping about in soggy clothes one's whole life.

Diomhair Caisteal adorned a steep cliff that towered over the ocean. Perhaps the castle's location had been selected to ward off invaders, but whichever long-dead laird had forced his subjects to construct the unsymmetrical compilation of turrets and towers had not needed to bother.

Miles was certain that no one, no matter how desperate, would want anything to do with this region. Even Vikings, who had the misfortune of being born in Denmark, or worse yet, Norway, had preferred to pillage the area in the summer, and row the long journey back, than attempt to live here.

Miles guided his horse into the hamlet, thankful he recalled the way. One would think that after existing for so many centuries, it would have occurred to someone to make a good sign. Then again, visitors were likely an abstract concept for the inhabitants.

Stone cottages were scattered over hills so steep he wondered how anyone managed to walk here, much less live with any degree of permanency. The homes seemed to mirror the crumbling Hadrian's Wall he'd crossed on the way to this blasted country.

Narrow windows, the small size chosen perhaps to lessen the incessant chill, or simply out of exasperation of ever seeing anything resembling proper sunlight shine through them, dotted the buildings at wide intervals.

If Miles were his older brother, he would live anywhere else. Apartments in Paris were more advantageous, and Miles possessed sufficient pride of his English heritage, and outrage over the French conduct during the Napoleonic Wars, to not mull over such alternatives lightly.

A few locals peered at him with suspicion. He wondered whether they could sense his Englishness. Likely he needed to scowl more vigorously to blend in.

A figure rushed down the hill. Mud clung to her hem,

and her cheeks were pink. She looked around frantically, but then smiled when she spotted him.

She cupped her hands to her mouth, and hollered, "Beggin' your pardon, sir. Are you the baron?"

She must work for the castle.

Good old Gerard, sending servants out despite the inclement weather, just on the off chance that he might be arriving. "I am!"

And she'd called him a baron too. His brother must be proud of Miles's new title, bestowed for his articles composed from war ravaged regions. Normally people reserved the title of baron for letters written on glossy parchment and bound with ornate wax seals.

The maid beamed and then dipped into a quick curtsy that seemed out of place on the craggy cliff.

"Ah, you needn't do that—" He started to say, as she said, "You need to come with me—"

His eyebrows soared upwards. His experience of maids was mostly confined to hearing the sound of rapidly scurrying feet when he entered a room or woke as they finished lighting a fire.

The maid's cheeks flushed, but she looked at him defiantly. "You are already late, I'm afraid."

Late?

He'd left the posting inn early.

His horse's speed might not be able to equal that of four strong horses, but at least his horse wasn't carrying a two-storied coach.

"I'm to inform you that you're wanted in the chapel," the maid continued, oblivious to her blatant insult at his tardiness-avoidance abilities.

"Everyone is there?"

"Everyone who should be there." She smiled. "My mistress looks very pretty."

"I'm not surprised." He shook his head. He still wasn't accustomed to the fact that his very rugged, adamantly roguish brother had married the woman most skilled at following the teachings of the *ton*. His sister-in-law always appeared splendid, but there was a reason everyone had once called her Ice Queen.

Fortunately Lady Rockport now seemed less stringent, but he had to confess, he'd expected to see Gerard end up with some equally wild Scotswoman, if he deigned to marry at all.

How the great are felled.

No matter.

He would visit his brother, use the castle as a base to find this anonymous authoress, and then he'd be back reporting decent stories. He followed the maid up the slope, leading his horse on the narrow path.

Perhaps his brother had taken the other guests on a walk, and they'd stopped to admire the stained-glass windows. Heavens knew there wasn't anything else to do in this region. No gentlemen's clubs, and certainly no cricket grounds.

The chapel was closer than the castle. This was good news. "I'll follow you."

"My mistress will be so happy."

His sister-in-law's perfectionist tendencies were renowned. No wonder she struggled with not knowing his precise arrival time.

He smirked. "I like to make an entrance."

The maid's lips twitched. "Then pardon if I say so, but I think you'll be quite well-suited."

He blinked. Was she still speaking about Gerard's wife?

Before he could question the maid, she pressed her hand against the heavy wooden door of the chapel, and he followed her into the dimly lit space. He'd expected a bevy of voices. Gerard had invited their brother Marcus, who'd hauled his whole extended family on the visit.

Miles's lips twitched. He could only surmise that Marcus had led his wife's sister's family here in order to curtail their visit. Marcus had always been clever, and the Scottish Highlands must contain all manner of wolf-dwelling caves and sharp drop-offs with which to scare one's American relations.

The chapel smelled of candle wax and dust, and he followed the maid through the dark room.

He bumped his foot against a wall and swore.

*

"Bloody hell." A deep, appealing baritone uttered the curse, and it echoed through the chapel.

The words themselves were unpleasant. In fact, few utterances could be less appropriate, but joy still cascaded through Veronique.

He's here.

She stepped toward the masculine figure struggling through the shadows.

Personally she would have selected a more laudatory word when entering a chapel. Something about the elaborate carvings, or even some compliment on the stained glass, though they were likely more striking when the weather lacked this magnitude of grimness.

But then, it could be no real surprise that the baron might make use of a wide vocabulary.

Veronique knew. She'd been corresponding with the man for the past two years. He might be Austrian, but the man was intelligent.

Her heart pattered, nervous despite the fact she knew him well.

Anyway. His appearance didn't matter. They had a greater, spiritual connection, one that couldn't be swayed by unsymmetrical faces or unduly bushy brows.

Love was the greatest force in the world, and after years of waiting, longing, imagining a love of her own, she'd found him.

She smoothed her hair, conscious of the slight tremble of her hands. Would he find her appealing?

She'd told him of her heritage in her last letter to him. For a few horrible minutes she'd worried he'd had second thoughts. European aristocrats did not tend to marry mulattos.

Most people assumed her to be of Southern European ancestry or thought her to be of the habit of forgoing bonnets and parasols. They didn't inspect her for signs of wide noses and overly thick, overly curly hair, but if the *ton* resembled any strata of American society, they would not be welcoming were they to discover her mother had descended from Barbadosian sugar pickers.

But it was Lord Braunschweig. The man who'd contacted her after reading her books, enthralled by every aspect of her life, patiently responding to each letter.

How could she ever have doubted his arrival?

She knew his thoughts, and the sound of his footsteps comforted her.

The man was so knowledgeable, writing on different

types of grains and farming seasons. A man filled with fervor on issues of cultivation practices must possess extraordinary zeal for more conventionally passionate subjects. He'd sought her out and then answered her every letter, writing pages back with regularity. He was the only person in the world, besides her stepsisters, aware of her secret.

It didn't matter what he looked like.

I love him.

She smiled at the familiar thought.

She craned her neck in the direction of his footsteps, and only the vicar's stern gaze prevented her from leaping into the newcomer's arms.

"I hope you are not the baron," the vicar boomed, his voice clearly accustomed to barreling through the room. His glower likely mimicked his expression when occupied with admonishing his flock for not donating sufficiently to the church.

"I am." Veronique's fiancé coughed. "Sorry about the—er—curse. It's dashed dark in that room. You should keep the door open."

His accent was impeccable. The man was so intelligent.

"And increase my susceptibility to catching a cold?" The vicar roared.

Footsteps sounded, and her heart halted.

This was it.

He stepped toward her, and her eyes rose from the man's Hessians, somewhat roughened from the harsh outside weather to tight buckskin breeches that hardly hid elegantly shaped thighs. The buttons on his high-collared tailcoat gleamed, but they could not succeed at distracting her from his perfect features, chiseled and masculine and utterly exquisite.

"My sweet darling," she said.

She'd never used this particular endearment before, and the baron blinked. He even looked behind him, as if she might be addressing another man.

She smiled.

He needn't worry.

There'd only ever been him, and now she would ensure that there would only be him for all eternity.

She stepped toward him, and she smiled as his green eyes widened.

"Do you like my dress?" She spun so the silver threads sparkled in the flickering candlelight.

"It's rather nice," he said. "Stunning in fact."

She beamed.

"And—er—rather fancy."

"This is a fancy occasion," she reminded him.

The most special occasion in our entire lives.

He looked around. "I expected to see my brother here. And his wife."

"You invited them?" She clapped her hands. Any last doubt he might be wary of her mother's background vanished. "They haven't arrived yet."

He nodded.

"We'll wait for them," she said.

"Good." His eyes flickered over her again.

Men's gazes had a tendency to dwell over her form. Something about the curves, which she'd heard described as luscious.

Until they realized...

She shook her head. The baron was made of sterner stuff. Though she'd worried—slightly, when he'd failed to appear, concerned he might have second doubts, given her...background, it was obvious worrying had been foolish.

He was her fiancé, her mate for eternity. Of course he would show up.

And soon he'll be my husband.

The vicar cleared his throat, the gesture made noisier by the absolute absence of any guests. "Shall we proceed?"

She glanced at her husband-to-be. He'd looked so adorably bewildered when he'd entered and had murmured about his family. If they were coming, Veronique would wait longer for the sacred sacraments, no matter how much the vicar frowned.

She shook her head. "We will wait for this man's family members. I'm sure they'll be here soon."

Her fiancé looked relieved.

"In that case I will get my greatcoat," the vicar said. "I have no confidence in this man's family's ability to be on time."

The baron's expression clouded. "I hope you are not insulting my relatives. Their importance cannot be overstated. Insulting a marquess and marchioness is inadvisable."

The vicar's stern face wobbled. "Forgive me, my lord. I was unaware your family was so important."

"I find that impossible to believe," the baron said firmly.

The vicar seemed prepared to argue, but he shook his head. "Forgive me. I am merely fetching my greatcoat."

Pride soared through Veronique at the sound of the vicar's newly meek voice. Her fiancé might not be battling an actual dragon, as in *Prince Delightful and the Dragon*, but he rivaled that hero in valiance. The baron's muscles curved under his coat, and Veronique supposed if he were confronted with an actual dragon, he would be equally successful at battling it.

"I am so happy you are here," she murmured, as the vicar tromped away. "You are even more marvelous than I imagined."

The baron's lips curled into a seductive smile. "Have you been thinking much of me?"

"You know I have."

He smirked.

The door slammed, and doubt ushered through Veronique. Perhaps she should have told her family about the wedding. Most of Veronique's favorite books ended in elopements, and it had only seemed appropriate for Veronique to emulate some of the romance bestowed on those heroines.

Still, her family would be so pleasantly surprised when they realized Veronique had alleviated all their worries for her on her own.

"My family is staying at the castle," she told him.

"Mine are too!" He beamed at her.

This was going far better than she'd hoped. He'd not only arrived, but he'd arranged accommodation for his family.

She wasn't surprised they were staying at Diomhair Caisteal. There were no other places in this hamlet, and didn't all aristocrats know one another? Something about attending one of the same three boarding schools.

"Perhaps I should ask my maid to bring them?" she asked.

He shrugged. "Why not?"

The man's tone was restrained. Perhaps he was embarrassed he'd dragged his whole family all the way from London, and she hadn't even bothered to invite hers from a few yards away.

"Miss Smith?" she called.

Her maid came to her.

"Please be sure to invite my family now."

The maid dipped into a curtsy. "I'm happy for you."

Veronique smiled back, and the maid's cheeks pinkened before she scurried away.

Veronique's mother's background might be unconventional, and in the full light, Veronique's appearance was viewed with similar hesitation, but it didn't matter. The baron loved her.

She glanced at him again. The man was truly handsome. In her moments of doubt, Veronique had wondered whether he would be as appealing in person as in his letters.

"Perhaps we should sit?" She hated the uncertainty in her voice.

"Very well." He guided her into a pew and slid beside her. His eyes sparkled with humor.

It was one thing to write about handsome men, but it was another thing when faced with a paragon of masculinity in the flesh. He seemed comprised solely of broad shoulders and chiseled features and swooping, perfectly tousled black hair. It was good he hadn't had time to attire himself in full dress for their wedding: she likely would have swooned on the spot if he were peering at her with those smoldering eyes underneath the glossy brim of a round hat.

"I did not expect such good company in Scotland." His voice was warm and velvety sounding.

She'd been correct to commission this expensive

wedding dress. Seeing the pleasure in his gaze made it all worthwhile.

"You've managed to exceed my expectations as well," she admitted, and her heart warmed at the wonder that seemed to grow in the man's gaze.

Chapter Four

The chit was magnificent.

He could almost forgive his brother for having the audacity to reside in Scotland if he managed to bring guests like this to his estate.

She spoke in a faint accent he couldn't place, and even in the flickering candlelight of the chapel, her features seemed more exotic than the peaches-and-cream complexions the female members of the *ton* sported, when they were not dabbing themselves in French-imported rouge.

It was odd no chaperone was present, but then again, Scotland must not seem as perilous as London's ballrooms. Manor house parties tended to have relaxed rules, something Miles on multiple occasions had cherished.

Foreign chits were splendid, much less stuffy than their English equivalents. Clearly the urge that had compelled them to cast off the yokes of British regulations in taxpaying denoted a looser adherence to etiquette and propriety.

He cursed himself for ever thinking uncharitable thoughts about his brothers' vast array of in-laws.

He glanced around, but the minister had not returned. Miles was no fool. This was his chance.

He grinned and put his hand over hers. This was an occasion for carpe diem. He expected her to tense, but she only smiled.

That beam. Painters would give their purses for an opportunity to portray such beauty. He longed to trace the curve of her sultry, full lips with his own.

"I am perhaps being forward," he murmured, "but you are utterly delightful."

He brushed his fingers over hers, luxuriating in the touch of her skin.

Normally high society women swathed their hands in gloves, unconcerned by the rough texture of the lace fabric.

Her embroidered gown shimmered. Perhaps Lady Rockport had arranged a ball for tonight. He wouldn't put it past his brother's wife.

"Your dress is beautiful." He noted the adorable manner in which her cheeks darkened. Had few men given her compliments before? *Outrageous.* He steadied his tone. "*You* are beautiful."

"Thank you." Her voice was soft and sultry and all parts of Miles soared to life.

"May I kiss you?" His heart caught, as if bracing himself for her rebuke. Even though they'd never met before, even though this was a chapel, it seemed vital she say yes.

She gave him a coy glance. "I thought you would never ask."

Heavens. She was remarkable.

He ran his hand against her hair, the locks curlier than that of most women he knew. The brown of her eyes seemed the loveliest color in the world, and for a moment he simply gazed at her.

His heartbeat galloped, as if he were still racing through the Highlands, though this time he was not evading storm clouds, but hastening toward the most exquisite sight.

He brushed his lips against hers. They were soft and succulent and just cold enough to jolt him further awake.

He pulled her toward him, conscious of her faint scent of vanilla, and they melted together.

She moaned, and he smiled, wrapping her in his arms.

She shivered against him. He wouldn't let her be cold, not when he was here, and he halted their kiss. His heartbeat thumped blissfully in his chest, and he removed his coat and draped it around her shoulders.

"Here you go," he said.

She looked surprised. "You don't want to admire my dress more? My seamstress would be disappointed."

"Your seamstress is not here, and I do not desire you to catch cold." He pulled her hands in his. "Now where were we?"

"Before you displayed such gallantry?" Her eyes were lively and intelligent. There was nothing rigid or repressed about her.

She hadn't remarked on his fame yet, and he trusted her to not have some impoverished, titled father hiding in the corner, eager to witness him compromising his daughter and display feigned anger, to ensure Miles would take her off his hands.

He kissed her again, this time more slowly, more deeply, more...thoroughly.

"Just like in my dreams," she murmured in that same throaty tone that caused havoc over his heart.

He was good at kissing.

Kissing was one of his favorite things to do.

Still, he'd never taken such pleasure in it before. Her lips moved somewhat awkwardly to begin with, despite the fact she'd hardly seemed to be taken aback by his suggestion.

But any hesitation soon vanished, and she followed him quickly and assuredly.

He kept his eyes closed, but only she consumed his thoughts.

The day might have started poorly, but it couldn't have ended any better. He leaned closer to her, clasping her within his arms.

A door creaked, and heavy footsteps thudded down the nave.

"What is this?" A male voice with a distinct American accent boomed behind him. "Veronique, honey. Are you fine?"

A female voice wailed. "Scandal! Scandal! She's been taken by a Highlander!"

"Not a Highlander," another voice said more coolly.

Gerard?

Miles stiffened, conscious his brother was here. Disapproval seemed to emanate through the man's voice, and Miles had never been more conscious of their age difference.

He glanced at the maid. *Of course.*

The woman—Veronique—pulled away from him.

He expected horror to be on her face at being so blatantly discovered. Instead she only smiled. "They're here. I'll introduce you."

Even women who attempted to compromise men feigned sorrow at being discovered.

She rose. "Hello, Papa." She smiled down at Miles. "Please let me introduce my family to you."

Family?

He jumped to his feet.

Family was not an exaggeration. Astounded faces, some whom he recognized, stared at them. Both his brothers, Marcus and Gerard, stood before him. Their wide-eyed faces were mirrored by their wives'.

The chapel was anything but empty now.

"Papa," Veronique said, her voice strong. "May I please introduce my fiancé to you?"

Fiancé?

"You're engaged, honey?" Her father frowned. "To some coatless scoundrel?"

"We should never have taken her to Scotland," the woman beside him mourned. "Disaster has struck!"

"Just my brother." Gerard directed a stern expression at Miles. "Please accept my utmost apologies."

"Apologies?" The woman wailed. "My stepdaughter has been compromised!"

Miles stiffened at the word. His brothers' faces paled. They knew what such an accusation meant—marriage, with a stranger.

"We shouldn't be overhasty," Marcus said finally. "I doubt she's with child."

"His coat was off," the older woman mourned, her voice louder and more strident than even the most passionate minister could be.

Any moment villagers might storm the chapel to discover the cause of the commotion.

He glanced uneasily at Veronique, but she seemed thoroughly unconcerned.

"Don't worry," she whispered. "They'll calm down soon."

He gazed warily at her parents. Calming down did not seem a possibility in the next five decades.

"You mustn't worry," Veronique said. "I know him."

Miles blinked.

"I assure you that he's quite suitable," Veronique continued.

Miles glanced at his family members, wondering if he might have misheard her. They looked similarly startled, and he despised the suspicion they directed at him.

Veronique's father's shoulders relaxed, even as Miles's shoulders rose.

Had this all been some horrible plan to seduce him after all?

Veronique stood. "Rise, dearest."

He stumbled upward, still taken aback.

"We are betrothed. He's a baron."

Betrothed?

"A baron?" Her parents looked somewhat less horrified.

"We were just about to wed," Veronique said.

"No," Miles croaked, his voice hoarse.

Chapter Five

Veronique stared at the man whom she'd just been embracing.

What on earth did he mean?

She'd corresponded with him for two years.

Nothing brought her more joy than another letter from him.

They'd planned to wed for months.

The baron had exuded confidence, but his face seemed paler, and his eyes seemed to have enlarged.

He gaped at her and then pulled his chiseled features into an expression that verged toward the accusatory. "Of course I'm not your bloody fiancé."

She stiffened at the curse.

This is not good.

Her heartbeat quickened, and the room swirled about her.

"But—" She stammered. "We exchanged so many letters! Y-you told me you loved me. You agreed to meet me here. You even brought your family!"

"My family is here." The man gestured to Lord and Lady Rockport. "They *live* here."

Heat invaded her face.

She'd been so happy. Joy had skipped through her veins, pulsating through her.

And this was...some stranger?

"I suppose he's not really a baron," Papa huffed. "Damned English bastards. Saying anything to seduce pretty girls. Don't worry, we'll hush this up." He glanced around the chapel and strode toward the vicar. "I can see you need some repairs to this church. This whole place could use a fresh coat of paint."

"Fresh paint!" the vicar stammered. "This is a medieval church. The oldest of its kind in the Highlands. I assure you no one will be going anywhere near this building with paint."

"Ah. Reckon you're wanting a more expensive bribe." Papa removed his purse. "What sort of things do you like? Statues? Paintings? Relics?"

The vicar raked a hand through thinning hair. "I suppose there might be something you could do."

"There always is," Papa said gaily. "Haven't met a man I couldn't bribe yet."

The vicar's face whitened. "I wouldn't use that particular word..."

"Just saying it like it is," Papa said. "No one becomes rich by wasting time. And I am, very, rich." He winked. "We'll doll this chapel up so it can take on the finest cathedral. Reckon the French would be willing to sell some of their takings from Italy and Spain to us, now that they're no longer an empire."

"We will not be taking anything from Catholics." The

minister lowered his voice, as if a bishop might pop up to berate him.

Veronique blinked hard. This was supposed to be her moment of triumph. Not a time for her father to brandish about his purse with the vigor of a medieval knight wielding a sword.

"See what you're making your poor, dear, lovely father do?" Her stepmother glowered. "What kind of trousseau do you expect to have if your father gives out all the money allotted to you before you even meet any real suitors?"

Veronique's throat dried. She glanced again at the baron. The man should have the decency to look ashamed.

"You kissed me!" she exclaimed. "You came here!"

"I'm ever so sorry." The maid flushed. "He told me he was the baron, miss."

Veronique hardened her gaze. "Are you telling me that you are not Lord Bertrand Braunschweig, Baron of Wolbert?"

"I am a baron," he said finally. "Though not Lord Braunschweig. This must be some sort of confusion. I am Lord Worthing."

Lord Worthing?

The name was familiar.

And then she blinked and dread rushed through her. "You're Lord Rockport's and Lord Somerville's younger brother."

"Yes," he said. "I came to visit. I'd just arrived when your maid found me and hauled me up here. That's why I asked if you'd seen my family."

Goodness.

She'd thought he was her fiancé. She'd—gracious, she'd kissed him. On the lips! What must he think of her?

What must Lord Braunschweig—her real fiancé—think if he knew?

"But you kissed me," she stammered.

He gave her a roguish grin. "So I did."

She'd been about to vow love and fidelity to one man, and had instead become intimate with another.

Heat surged through her, as if someone had set her aflame. Her limbs seemed to crumple, and she sank back onto the pew.

She glanced toward the door, as if Lord Braunschweig might be entering, but no one appeared.

"Hmph," Papa said. "Seems you made a mistake, Veronique, honey."

"But you're still a baron," her stepmother said thoughtfully, addressing Lord Worthing.

"I am," he said.

Veronique despised that the sound of his voice caused her heart to flutter. She'd been so certain everything would be perfect. She abhorred that the person who'd held her in his arms with such confidence, who'd made her heart soar and her lips swerve upward, was not actually Lord Braunschweig.

She shouldn't feel disappointed. Lord Braunschweig was better, and whatever kept him from being here must be worthwhile indeed.

"I haven't seen that dress before." Her stepmother frowned.

Drat.

"I commissioned it." She raised her chin, though she did shift her feet to hide her jeweled slippers.

Her stepsisters, Louisa and Irene, knew about her career, knew about the steady stream of income, but she'd kept the fact hidden from her father and stepmother.

The subject she wrote about was...sensitive.

"It's a beautiful dress, honey," Papa said. "Girl's got good taste."

Her stepmother strode toward her. "Is that silver thread?"

Veronique leaped up. "Why don't we go back to the castle?"

"You should probably give the man his coat," Papa said. "Doesn't look decent, finding you like this."

"With your tongues in each other's mouths," her stepmother added. "Most horrendous, Veronique. You've wounded us. Irreparably."

"I wouldn't say that, darling." Papa strode over the old cobble stone tiles, worn from centuries of people padding to the altar to pray.

"Hmm..." A strange look crossed over her stepmother's face, and for the faintest second, so short she couldn't be certain she'd witnessed it, her stepmother smiled.

What on earth was she thinking?

Her stepmother moved toward the baron in quick determined paces. "You compromised our daughter."

The baron's face paled, and he glanced at his brothers. "I—er—wouldn't say that. It was a kiss."

"A long, deep kiss," her stepmother said. "And your coat was off."

"Veronique was cold," the baron—the wrong baron—said.

"Miss Daventry, you mean," her mother declared, almost triumphantly.

Veronique knew her stepmother couldn't actually be triumphant, because what was there for her to be happy about?

Unless... Veronique shivered, and something in her stomach hardened.

She was so close to her dream.

Lord Braunschweig would arrive. She was certain. What in heavens was her stepmother doing?

But she knew.

"I think it's significant that you referred to her by her Christian name," her stepmother said.

"That was the only name I knew—"

Her stepmother raised a hand in the air. "You were compromising her."

The baron's face paled further. Not that the fact made him appear any less handsome.

"We found you in this building—this sacred space—alone." Her stepmother's eyes definitely gleamed now, and she placed her hand over her heart. "We were shocked and appalled to find my husband's only child, his sweet, innocent daughter in the throngs of an embrace with a person lacking basic clothes."

"Just my coat was off," the baron said quickly.

"Who knows what you had gotten up to before then?" Her stepmother glanced toward the altar. "We demand you wed her. She—she may be with child."

"That would be impossible," the baron said.

Her stepmother frowned. "You would say that. But how is she supposed to find a husband when we can no longer vouch for her purity?"

The baron had a stricken expression on his face. He turned to his brothers. "Marcus, Gerard—tell her this is nonsense."

Lord Somerville and Lord Rockport retained thoughtful expressions on their faces.

"Forgive me, Miles," Lord Somerville said finally. "But you were alone with her. Anything could have happened."

"But you saw everything that did," the baron stammered.

Veronique froze. This was supposed to be her wedding day. But not to this stranger.

The man was squirming at the thought of being forced to marry her. But she had no intention of allowing that to happen.

"I love another," she cried out. "Lord Braunschweig. I love Lord Braunschweig. W-we were going to wed today. That's why I had the maid fetch you."

Papa frowned. "I don't know that man. How did you meet him, honey?"

Veronique firmed her jaw. "We haven't met yet. But we've corresponded for the past two years."

She tucked a strand of hair behind her ear, remembering how he had written a letter to Mr. Simons to ask to be put in touch with her. He had sought her out. It wasn't the first time an admirer had.

She closed her eyes. All those beautiful long letters.

He loved her. She was certain. "He'll be here."

*

The only thing worse than being compromised, was to hear the chit in question begging her parents not to force her to marry him. It was damned embarrassing. Damned good of her, but embarrassing all the same.

He glanced at his brothers. Marcus and Gerard both had somber, shocked faces.

Miles closed his eyes.

She'd been so pretty and charming. How was he to

know she'd thought him someone else? Women were supposed to know what their own fiancés looked like.

But he understood. An entire ocean separated Britain and America. Only kings commissioned paintings of their foreign brides before agreeing to marry them, and even they couldn't depend on an honest portrayal.

Gerard and Marcus whispered together, and then Gerard strode to him.

"Hullo," Miles said.

"I see you arrived." Gerard didn't deign to give him a proper greeting.

"Er—rather." He raked a hand through his hair, conscious of his still missing tailcoat. He smoothed his sleeves, wrinkled from when he'd embraced Veronique, but Gerard's face darkened.

Miles scowled. Gerard shouldn't be giving him a hard time. His brother had gotten himself into scrapes before.

Except—was this really just a scrape? Even if Veronique—Miss Daventry—persuaded her parents not to marry him, hadn't he damaged her? A girl couldn't go on as normal if her parents found her in the arms of a strange man. The event must be dashed inconvenient for her.

He'd—he'd fancied her. More than he'd ever fancied anyone else. Ten minutes ago, their encounter had seemed magical.

This though could not be more miserable.

"Forgive me," he told his brother.

He hated the meekness in his tone. He was never meek.

Gerard didn't deign to give him a proper greeting. "You should marry her."

Horror swept through him. "You know how it is, Gerard. We were caught in the moment."

"This is a chapel," Gerard said sternly. "You can't go around kissing strange women in chapels."

"I—" Miles sighed. "You're right. I promise not to do it again."

"It didn't occur to ask her why she was eager to kiss you?"

Miles gave him a smug look. "Frankly, the only question I would have is why she *wouldn't* want to. My renown with women is considerable. They know about the prowess of...all my muscles."

"Miss Daventry is new to this country. Fresh from Massachusetts. How is she supposed to find a husband if there are rumors about her?"

"Then don't make rumors," Miles said.

"There were many witnesses." Gerard shook his head. "You should know better."

"You were a rogue once," Miles muttered. "One doesn't accidentally become *Matchmaking for Wallflowers' Rogue to Avoid*."

"Nor does one find oneself kissing a strange chit accidentally. I can't help you get out of this."

"You know I don't believe in marriage."

Gerard smiled. "Cordelia and I despised each other when we eloped."

Miles blinked.

"Miss Daventry is a pleasant girl. She seems intelligent. And you obviously find her pretty. Her father is wealthy. You could do worse."

"Out of the question," Miles said.

Marriage was something other men discussed, after an overindulgence in brandy, when they permitted themselves to ponder their favorite dance partner with ridiculous sentimentality. Marriage was something some men mulled over after seeing nephews or nieces of the particularly adorable variety.

Marriage was something Miles knew better than to contemplate.

He knew his parents. He knew how his mother had married the wrong person, causing havoc when she'd cavorted with Miles's father. He knew Gerard's father had died brokenhearted, and servants still spoke of the scandal of his mother's marriage to the man with whom she'd had an affair.

Miles was not going to make his mother's mistake. He refused to marry anyone. If he made no commitments, no one would get hurt. *Simple.*

He wasn't the oldest son. He had an estate, but it was small, and if Gerard's or Marcus's heirs inherited it after he died, so be it. His parents were dead, and he had no matchmaking mama to contend with.

"I see that you already found Scotland enticing," Gerard said.

The statement should have been innocuous.

Normally Miles would take it as a chance to mull over the less than ideal climate and encourage his brother to spend increased time in England.

He might even muse over the general unpleasantness of mail coaches with him. Gerard, he had thought, would sympathize with his experience with Miss Haskett.

The only emotion Gerard seemed to be conveying now was disapproval.

"I'm sorry," Miles said again.

"She is a guest of mine," Gerard said. "An innocent. This is her first time in the country. I would have thought I could have protected her in a hamlet from my own brother."

"Clearly I'm too much of a rake," Miles said.

"That is not a good thing," Gerard said.

"I seem to remember you being very proud of your roguish status."

"I was a fool," Gerard said. "And you are too."

"I'm going to tell you a secret," Gerard said. "Marriage is the best bloody thing in this world."

"Indeed?"

"Most certainly," Gerard said.

Miles frowned. He wondered where his brother was. The one who'd joined him at gaming halls and White's.

He wrapped his arms together.

He wasn't sure why he'd bothered to drive up this distance to see him. He should have devoted his time solely on finding Loretta Van Lochen. He sighed. "Perhaps you arranged for Miss Daventry to compromise me."

"Naturally not," Gerard said, his voice outraged.

More people turned to look at them.

He shook his head firmly. "I won't marry." He glanced at Veronique. "And I'm certain she has no desire to marry me either."

The vicar cleared his throat. "If there is to be no marriage, I suggest you take your arguing elsewhere. Some people in this hamlet still consider a chapel to be a place for prayer. I imagine that Lord Rockport's castle is sufficiently large for all of you to debate Miss Daventry's future further."

The other faces reddened, and they left the chapel.

Miles fetched his horse and led it toward the castle stables. The others made their way toward the castle, treading over the narrow path. Icy wind swept over Miles, as if reminding him he did not belong here.

He frowned as he stepped over the increasingly muddy trail.

The worst of it was, when he closed his eyes, he still remembered the brush of Veronique's lips against his own and the happy beat of his heart.

He tried to meet Veronique's gaze, but her stricken face hardly comforted him.

Perhaps, despite both their protestations, she would become his wife. Miles shuddered. He may not have been speaking, may not have formed the four-letter word on his tongue, but his face still contorted.

Miles wasn't supposed to be wed. He knew better than to succumb to morals touted by Bible toting clerics. Marriage was for other people, from more conventional families.

He'd been born of passion.

Wild, notorious passion.

Columnists had written about it, turning it into legend with an enthusiasm that only paralleled the real Guinevere.

Miles knew. He knew every time he introduced himself, and every time the person in question's eyebrows raised, head tilted, and lips drew into a smirk. He was the son who should have been a bastard, should have been a lovechild, somebody who should have been sent quietly to the front to protect the more important dukes and earls who were not born of scandal.

Everyone knew his mother, the incomparably beautiful Guinevere, had married the very mediocre appearing, yet wealthy Marquess of Highgate for his money. And everyone also knew she'd promptly asked him to build her a manor house in Kent and fallen for one of the local gentry there. Everyone knew she'd broken her husband's heart, and though not everybody was certain his fatal bout with bronchitis should be blamed on her, they all chided her careless disregard for her late husband.

His parents had bequeathed him with a clear complexion, chiseled features, and a propensity toward well-proportioned muscles that he readily put to good use. Women found his figure appealing, and Miles found women appealing.

Marriage was something that could be postponed, ideally forever. Marrying was decidedly off-limits. There had to be some advantages to being a younger son.

Miles had a reputation to maintain, even if both his brothers had inexplicably decided to settle into matrimony, abandoning their access to an incessant stream of sumptuous women. He rather thought his brothers' intelligence was vastly overrated.

He glanced at her.

And blinked.

They were outside, and somehow, under the stronger light, her features seemed even more...foreign.

Debutantes were not supposed to appear foreign. They were supposed to possess peaches-and-cream complexions. Some more unfortunate ones might have alabaster complexions, or if they were very unlucky, and possessed an aptitude for barging from their manor homes to wander in their gardens, freckles might be scattered over their faces.

But they were certainly not supposed to possess foreign features.

And Veronique most certainly seemed in possession of those characteristics.

Her nose was wider and flatter than that of the young

ladies he knew. Her hair was curly, but it was her skin that he devoted the most attention to.

It was dark.

Not very dark. But darker than any ladies of the *ton* he'd met before. He tilted his head. Her father certainly did not seem to have the same skin tendency.

Did that mean her mother was more dark?

He frowned.

Perhaps Massachusetts simply had lots of sun.

Or perhaps... Perhaps her mother was of Spanish heritage? Italian?

He frowned.

She almost appeared... He shook his head.

He was being too fascinated by her, seeing things that didn't make sense.

She was a foreigner, and it made sense that she might appear somewhat different from the English chits he knew, with their carefully maintained complexions through a well-practiced rejection of going outside without a deep brimmed bonnet and parasol.

And yet it must be true.

She was half African.

He looked at Miss Daventry again, but then glanced away quickly. If he looked at her, it was too easy to dwell on her features, and the soft curve of her waist. That would do no good. She was betrothed and not interested in him.

She wasn't the first person of African heritage he'd met. Not at all. Plenty of dark skinned people lived in London, their families residing here since the Romans arrived, but there were fewer in the depths of the Highlands.

Most of the ones he met were servants and

dishwashers, happy to no longer be slaves, perhaps brought by their masters to England, and happy to reside in a land where the slave trade was illegal.

There were rather fewer people of African heritage in higher society. Dido Belle had been raised by her uncle, an earl, as one of his own, but she'd died a few years ago.

Still...Veronique—Miss Daventry—was the stepsister of a duke. It was impossible for her to have any African blood.

Chapter Six

He hadn't appeared.

Veronique swallowed, conscious of the ridiculousness of her attire as they marched to the castle.

Today was supposed to be the most wonderful day of her life.

What had halted Lord Braunschweig's arrival?

Perhaps she'd been foolish to suggest they wed here. Though the Highlands were alluring, the steep slopes were difficult to reach.

Perhaps highwaymen had captured him or wolves had besieged him. Perhaps he lay in some ditch somewhere, reciting her letters to himself as he bled. Or perhaps he'd been taken ill, and was lying in his sick bed, at his home in London, the guilt of not meeting her making it impossible for him to recover.

Or perhaps he doesn't desire to marry me.

The thought tore at her heart.

Had her last letter scared him?

She wrapped her arms together. The gesture might not

be ladylike, but she didn't care. All she cared about was Lord Braunschweig.

I love him.

Perhaps it was foolish to love someone she'd never met, but they'd exchanged letters every week.

She knew what pudding he favored and his opinion on London. He was Austrian, new to the country just like she was, displaced during the war. He'd risen to the position of diplomat, working to make the world better. He was so wise, so intelligent. He'd even offered her advice on where she might invest some of her money.

No one knew her better than he did. The first time he'd written he'd loved her, she'd pressed the sheets of paper against her heart.

Her father and stepmother wouldn't allow her to dance with Salem's men, too worried they'd guess the truth about her heritage, but Lord Braunschweig cared for her. He hadn't even needed to meet her to fall in love with her.

He'd been her rock, her beacon for so long.

She would wait for him. He might not have showed up now, but he would. She was certain.

Her stepmother's anger had dissipated. Instead she was remarking on the husbanding skills of Lord Rockport and Lord Somerville, marveling at the baron's features and accomplishments, despite the fact Veronique had told her she loved another.

Suddenly the castle's proximity to a chapel did not seem like an advantage, nor did the fact that one didn't have to wait for the banns to be published before marrying in Scotland.

If her stepmother insisted she wed Lord Worthing, Veronique might struggle to resist.

"Lord Worthing is accomplished at riding," her

stepmother said. "I mentioned your enjoyment of the pastime."

"Everyone does."

Why wouldn't one want to sit upon a horse and allow it to take one all over the landscape?

They neared the castle. Perhaps Lord Braunschweig had gone straight there.

She beamed.

She'd told him the name of the castle, and many castles had chapels on site. It may not have occurred to him that the chapel could be located in the village.

Perhaps he was there now, pacing Diomhair Caisteal in distress, and casting melancholic glances at the horizon while quoting Byron.

She gazed at the castle, just in case she might see a person casting forlorn looks at the garden.

She smiled. The man would experience such joy when he saw her. Likely he would sweep her into his sturdy arms, thrust her on top of his white stallion and gallop with her to London and all things brilliant and romantic.

Veronique pushed away the memory of being in Lord Worthing's arms and the blissful sensations she'd experienced there

Perhaps Lord Worthing was in possession of regular features and a roguish grin, perhaps her heart had inadvertently pounded more beats than necessary in his presence, but he wouldn't compare to Lord Braunschweig, because it was Lord Braunschweig whom she loved.

They approached the castle doors, and Veronique's heart rate quickened. The butler opened the door, and the others marched into the hallway, thrusting their great coats and pelisses at the servants.

She waited for the butler to mention a guest.

But the man didn't.

She wrapped her coat more tightly around her. She didn't want to look down and see her beautiful sparkling silk dress. She felt foolish in it. It was meant for Lord Braunschweig.

Her stepmother cleared her throat. "Veronique, you must marry Lord Worthing."

The man's shoulders slumped.

"It's the correct thing to do," her stepmother continued. "It's the honorable thing. I'm certain that Lord Rockport wouldn't have invited a dishonorable man into such close contact with our daughter."

Anger shot through Veronique. She should stifle it, should perhaps excuse herself to go upstairs. She absolutely shouldn't respond, not with everyone here.

But she had to say something.

"Lord Worthing and I do not love each other," she said.

Her stepmother snorted. "You've only just met. You should see your lack of love for each other as a favorable sign that neither of you are mad."

Veronique tensed.

She could walk out of here now. She had the funds to provide for herself, even if it might be too shocking to admit the fact to anyone.

There was a reason she had not confided her profession to her stepmother.

Her stepmother had a well-developed sense of propriety, strengthened ever since Percival unexpectedly became a duke.

Money making was an occupation best left to the very lowest classes of women who had no other recourse but to wash floors and beat rugs to avoid sending their sons up sooty chimneys.

"Perhaps Lord Worthing might be interested in learning about my life," Veronique said sweetly.

Her stepmother cast a worried glance at Veronique's father.

"Where were you born, Lord Worthing?" Veronique asked, addressing him for the first time since they'd left the chapel. "Shall I tell you where I was born?"

Looking at the baron was a mistake.

It was too easy to go from there to remembering the feel of his arms about her waist and his kisses on her lips.

She moved her gaze away, hoping her cheeks were not flushed.

Her stepmother laughed, though the sound was hollow. "Lord Worthing would not be interested in where you were born, my dear. He's much more concerned about where you will live. Perhaps your father might be able to put some money toward a townhouse in London." She addressed the baron. "Tell me, Lord Worthing, what is your favorite section of London. Grosvenor Square? St. James?"

Veronique raised her chin. "Both are quite different from where I was raised."

"I've always been interested in visiting Boston," Lord Worthing said, and then his face reddened. Perhaps he thought she might think him eager to marry her.

She smiled at him. He was the first person she'd met in England who'd expressed an interest in her home state, and then she remembered what she needed to tell him.

Her throat dried, her stepmother's ever deepening frown not reassuring.

Veronique told herself her past wasn't important.

It shouldn't be important.

What did her grandmother have to do with her now?

Especially when her grandmother was the kindest person she'd ever known? But she'd never forget the comments of the servants when she'd first moved in with her father in Massachusetts. She'd never forget the whispers on the streets whenever she'd walked on her own. And she'd never forget how her stepmother had finally announced that she should not be brought with them to balls and events, lest she damage the marriage prospects of her two stepsisters.

Veronique sighed.

Maybe Lord Worthing would be horrified enough by her past that he would resolve not to be persuaded to marry her, no matter how much coin her father flung.

That would be good, then she could marry Lord Braunschweig. *Bertrand.*

She pushed away the ever-growing fear that the reason he hadn't appeared was that he'd had doubts about being married to a mulatto.

She shook her head.

Bertrand loved her. He'd told her in his letters. She couldn't allow herself to forget that.

"Lord Worthing should learn the truth."

Her stepmother emitted an unsteady laugh. "Nonsense, dear."

Her father sighed. "Your stepmother is correct. We agreed not to do so."

"But he might marry me." She glanced at Lord Worthing. The man's face had blanched further.

She gave a wry smile. Likely the man's surprise would only strengthen.

"There's something you should know about me." Veronique addressed him.

"Darling—" Her father attempted to protest, but she wouldn't let him.

She raised her hand. "I owe him this knowledge."

"I was born in the West Indies," she continued. "On Barbados."

Her parents glowered, but it didn't matter. Lord Worthing deserved to know.

"My father hadn't made his fortune yet—"

"Or his sense," her stepmother muttered.

Veronique cleared her throat. "So when my father saw someone...unsuitable—"

"Whom I loved," her father cut in, and she smiled.

"He had a child with her. Me."

Lord Worthing nodded. He hadn't drawn his brows together, and he hadn't tilted his head, as if reflecting on the skin tones and nose shapes of other women.

She inhaled. "I'm mulatto."

There was a stunned silence, and she felt everyone's eyes on her. Even Lord Rockport and Lord Somerville, who'd both seemed the very definition of calm and imperturbable widened their eyes.

Her stepmother shifted her legs, obviously uncomfortable. "On her mother's side. I'm really not certain that matters."

The others nodded at the lie.

It did matter.

If it hadn't mattered, then they never would have urged her to keep it secret. If it hadn't mattered, they'd have permitted her to attend social gatherings and balls in Massachusetts, and not hidden her away, lest her heritage embarrass her father and his new wife.

"You don't appear mulatto," Lady Somerville said.

Her voice wasn't skeptical, more puzzled.

Veronique sighed. "You don't know what to look for. My skin isn't that dark, but my nose is still too wide, and my hair is too curly."

"I think you look beautiful," Lady Somerville said, and the others quickly assented.

They were polite and kind, but the rest of society did not tend to replicate those emotions.

"I—er—trust you'll all keep this secret," her stepmother said.

The others nodded vigorously.

"I think you should retire," her stepmother told her, and Veronique nodded.

She glanced at Lord Worthing, but he only gave her a bland smile, as if he'd somehow known already.

"I was born in Kent," he said. "Fewer palm trees."

She nodded. "Oh."

What had she thought, confessing all that?

She'd loved her childhood on Barbados. If only the memories of her grandmother were not clouded with the knowledge that she would be seen as everything improper by everyone Veronique knew today.

If only Lord Braunschweig had shown up.

She quelled the thought that she had told Lord Braunschweig about her West Indian connection, and he'd abandoned her at the altar.

That couldn't be the reason, could it?

He'd loved her. He'd told her.

He'd started writing her after reading her books. He'd showered compliments on her, begging her to marry him once he'd found out her age and unmarried status.

It had been a true meeting of the minds, of the spirits, unconcerned with anything else.

If he had wanted to marry her when he hadn't even met

her, surely that would be the case no matter what her skin color was. Love was the strongest thing in the world.

But if she didn't find Lord Braunschweig, she might be compelled to marry Lord Worthing.

The thought was atrocious, and she hurried from the Great Hall to her bedroom upstairs. Tears prickled her eyes, and she gazed out her narrow window. The Highlands soared before her. Beyond the steep inclines was England, and then...London, the most magnificent city in the world, where slavery was illegal, and she would be content with her true love.

She stared outside, hoping to see a horse rider making his way toward the castle over the hills, underneath the setting sun.

Pink and orange danced over the horizon, but the only creatures they illuminated were some sheep and goats.

He's not coming.

Veronique paced the room. Normally when upset she might throw herself into writing tales of wild adventures, of heroes clattering up castle walls or swinging from vines.

She paused and glanced outside.

An idea struck her, and for the first time that evening she smiled.

Chapter Seven

No thunderstorms hammered rain and lightning onto the Highlands, no thieves clambered over the castle walls, rousing the inhabitants, and no roosters, belonging to some farmer, crowed.

Miles should have slept well.

He should still be sleeping.

The brick in his bed had cooled, and he tossed underneath the plentiful covers laid over him.

Thoughts of the blissful sensation of Veronique's lips against his, followed by the realization that she'd mistaken him for someone else and he might be forced to wed a stranger tore through his mind.

Sleep seemed frivolous.

Today might be his wedding day.

He smiled as he recalled Veronique's spirited statement on her birth. He hadn't known it was possible for so many people to be so quiet. He'd recognized her ethnicity, but he wasn't surprised that the others, who'd traveled less, had only seen what they'd expected to see.

Veronique was more interesting than any woman he'd ever met.

Miss Daventry, he reminded himself.

A creaking noise interrupted his thoughts, and curiosity swept through him.

He stepped onto the cold floorboards. Anything to distract himself from musing over Veronique. It didn't matter how good her lips had felt against his own. She desired this Lord Braunschweig person, and Miles intended to never marry.

He remembered wandering Rockport Manor as a child, conscious of the strange portraits of his mother with another gentleman, and of a half-brother who'd lost his father.

Passion was pleasant, but it was best confined to short doses.

Another creak sounded.

Somebody was on the balcony.

Had Lord Braunschweig arrived after all? Perhaps he'd decided to surprise Veronique.

Miles crept to the balcony door, maneuvering past heavy Scottish furniture and medieval suits of armor. He pushed aside velvet curtains.

The castle sat on a steep cliff that towered over the ocean. A murky moat separated the castle from the surrounding land, and though Miles doubted actual alligators lurked in the moat, as depicted in the illustrations in his nephews' children's books, he had no desire to topple into the inky waters.

Gerard could extol the castle, but Miles remained unimpressed. He lived in Sussex, surrounded by modern manor homes with large windows and facades formed by something besides the indiscreet pummeling of harsh weather.

Only some birds seemed to be outside, resting on the stone ledge, and Miles almost reentered his room.

Then he saw a long white object hanging from another window. It was so thin, for a moment he thought it part of the architecture.

Even this castle shouldn't have fabric billowing from the side. Even Scottish traditions couldn't be so absurd.

He frowned. Perhaps a servant had draped a sheet from the window?

He didn't think so. There would be other places to dry laundry besides flinging it alongside the rocky, dirty wall of a medieval castle.

A figure appeared at the window, and Miles's chest constricted.

Surely the person couldn't be attempting to climb down the castle wall?

But someone did appear to be clambering down the white fabric, which he realized were sheets tied together.

Bloody hell.

It was Veronique.

The chit was escaping.

She hadn't wanted to marry him. He'd seen her face whiten when she realized he was a different baron.

And now she was venturing into the muddy, Scottish terrain to go to her fiancé.

Damnation.

Curses had never seemed so suitable to Miles. He couldn't let her roam Britain alone. Who knew what harm might happen to her? She was a foreigner and a woman.

Most people of their class didn't even like their women

to travel without a servant. Definitely no servant was following her. No one in their right mind would.

He called from the window. "Halt! Halt!"

If she heard him, she didn't stop. In fact she seemed to be doing the very opposite of stopping. She slid down the sheets easily, pulling the fabric between her hands as her feet touched the wall.

Good   . What was he supposed to do? Let her continue? And risk all manner of harm to her? Did she distrust him so much that risking her life was better than marrying him?

I have to stop her.

He was still in his nightshirt, and he hastily dressed, choosing the warmest items his valet had packed.

He should write a note, but he didn't have time. She was running away too quickly. Once she reached the stables, it would be much more difficult to catch up with her. He needed to bring her back to the castle.

He stepped onto the ledge, and his greatcoat billowed in the wind.

Damnation.

He glanced at the departing figure. The only good thing one could say about Veronique—Miss Daventry—was that she'd not headed toward the ocean.

Lady Rockport's brother, the Duke of Belmonte and his bride professed a strong love for the sea. Miles had no similar idealistic impressions of the largest deathtrap in the world.

Not that running into the depths of the Highlands was a vast improvement. He tried to think about if the Highlands had any deadly bogs and marshes.

Never mind.

He'd nab her quickly.

He'd evaded French spies in the war. He smirked. What was a thirty-foot wall?

*

Veronique missed Massachusetts, and the abundant maple and elm trees that bestowed conveniently perched branches to climb.

Perhaps fleeing had been an imperfect idea.

She sighed.

She hadn't spent two years corresponding with Lord Braunschweig to abandon him.

Whatever prevented him from arriving must be important, and if so, she needed to help him.

The bank account her stepbrother Arthur had opened for her on his last visit to the United States was not empty. She'd seen the surprise on the banker's face at the ever-increasing amount of money. She'd invested it, growing her wealth further.

Money brought comfort to her. Perhaps women were expected to marry to secure their fortunes, but she couldn't depend on that. Men might find her appearance pleasing, but that didn't mean they desired their unborn children to take on her skin tone.

Her stepmother had warned her to expect men to only desire her as a mistress. Men might find her appearance alluring and wish to see her splayed on their ivory sheets, but finding a man to marry her, actually marry her, and not merely ensconce her in some city flat which he visited whenever his own wife and children grew tiresome, might be an unreasonable aspiration.

She refused to abandon Lord Braunschweig and

padded over the soggy ground. Mud, formed from rivulets of melting snow, squished around her boots.

She slowed as she neared the flat stone building. Did the groomsmen sleep here? She would have to be quiet. She prayed the horses would be similarly restrained.

The stable doors were locked.

Drat.

Her heart thudded, and she glanced back at the castle. Dark gray turrets, the stone seemingly chosen for its ability to resemble menacing storm clouds, stabbed the sky, and the tied together sheets from her window billowed in the wind, unhampered with her absence.

A dark form clambered down the wall, and she gasped.

The man moved lithely over the stone, his muscles strong enough to grip the rocky surface, and his feet sure enough to not lose his balance.

There was only one reason for someone to descend the steep castle wall in so eccentric a manner.

I'm being followed.

Outrage coursed through her. Lucinda in *The Princess in the Tower* never had to deal with a person following her when she'd made her escape in Chapter Fifteen.

She refused to allow someone to stop her now. She scoured the ground for a rock, and then, when she'd found one, smashed a window.

Horses neighed, and she forced away the smattering of guilt. Lord Rockport could afford a new pane.

She crushed the last glass with her stone and climbed through the window.

The air inside the stables was mustier, the scent imbued with animals and dust and hay and...other things. Her nostrils flared involuntarily, and she hurried past stalls until she found Graeme, a calm, older horse whom she'd ridden earlier.

Graeme was perhaps not quite the fierce stallion that Lucinda had taken in *The Princess in the Tower*, but though Lord Rockport likely had more pedigree-filled horses, she didn't trust her ability to place a saddle on a strong steed, much less ride it.

So Graeme it would be.

At least she knew how to put a saddle on the horse. Writing *The Stallion of Spain* had taught her that.

Veronique gave a longing glance at the side saddle, but selected one of the masculine variety. A mail coach could take her most of the way to London, but it was important to have a saddle she was unlikely to become stuck in, no matter how strong her preference for riding in a ladylike manner.

She picked up the saddle and scampered to Graeme's stall. There were some advantages to an older horse, and he seemed to not think it an indignity to have a leather object forced over him.

She guided the horse from the stall and mounted him. She felt tall and ready for anything.

She thought of the figure of a man clambering down the wall. She must have imagined him, though perhaps she truly would need to be prepared for anything.

Veronique wrapped the cloak more tightly around her and urged Graeme to the road that led to the village.

The castle was even lovelier in the distance. It was more imposing, and the outline looked almost threatening against the gray sky.

I'm in Britain.

She'd spent so many years dreaming about the country, and now she was finally here. She refused to spend her time confined in a castle with her matchmaking stepmother.

Not when there was a perfectly good baron who adored her.

The snow seemed thicker away from the coast, and the sunrays cast a tangerine and pink glow over the once white slabs. Veronique's fingers itched to grab her quill to record the moment, but she couldn't allow anyone the chance to find her.

Once she reached the nearest posting inn, she would be able to board a mail coach.

And then she would see Lord Braunschweig, and their spirits would be united.

Chapter Eight

M iles swore.
He may have climbed mountains in Switzerland, but he'd never expected to clamber down a wall in Scotland. He gripped his hand onto the cold, rough stone. At least Gerard's ancestors hadn't decided to haul smooth slabs of limestone from Normandy. The wind slammed against his body, and he willed his fingers to not freeze as he moved downward.

Some people who climbed advocated not looking down, but Miles never subscribed to that belief. Looking down was the best part: it was the closest he could come to actually flying, and he inhaled the crisp air, tinged with salt from the ocean. Waves swept onto the rocky shore, moving in a regular rhythm, as if in an incessant show of strength.

He descended the tower, finally landing on the soggy ground. He rounded the moat and then sprinted across the stone bridge.

Veronique should be looking at him in awe. Scaling a castle wall was not a task for everyone.

The chit had vanished, and he shouted her name. Maybe if he roused people, they would help him search for her.

The gales drowned his shouts, and he scowled.

He tramped his way through thick, uncut grass. Gerard needed to get the farmers to have their sheep graze here.

No woman should travel alone, but especially not one as pretty, yet distinctive looking as Veronique. Pondering all the problems that might befall her would be an interminable task.

Returned soldiers roamed the country, their minds plagued by demons, and their bodies fed irregularly. Britain hadn't coped well with the sudden surge of young men. There weren't jobs, and Miles didn't want to ponder what might occur if one of them happened across a naïve woman.

British skies had a dreadful habit of pouring rain at frequent intervals, and huge puddles sat on paths even when it wasn't raining. Wild animals roamed the territory, terrorizing even those travelers who hadn't gotten lost in the landmarkless landscape, devoid of proper buildings.

Miles sprinted toward the stables. Two people who'd managed to sneak down steep castle walls would be able to find their way back inside, even if returning meant using the actual front door and bribing the butler to not gossip about their entrance.

The door was open, and he entered the stable. Hay crunched beneath his feet. "Miss Daventry!"

A few horses neighed in response, and his heart sank. *Bloody hell.*

He counted the horses, but one stall was empty.

That chit.

He inhaled. He could go back to the castle and rouse the others—but time was of the utmost importance.

He took a muscular appearing horse, strapped a saddle on its back and led it from the stables.

Rain drizzled, and he scowled. He'd better find her soon. He leapt onto the horse and urged it forward.

England was south, and when he came to a fork in a road, he didn't hesitate which trail to choose.

He directed his horse down the road that led from the castle, winding around a steep hill.

A thought occurred to him. If he clambered up the hill, it would provide him with a vista suitable for spotting a woman riding on a fast-moving horse.

Miles sighed and urged his horse to still. The horse whinnied, athletic enough to find the process of standing less favorable to that of galloping. Perhaps he should have selected a horse in possession of a lower propensity to rush about. He soothed the horse and tied it to one of the gnarly bushes that dotted the estate.

He scrambled up slippery granite and mud, grasping onto moss, until he'd finally hauled himself to the top of the peak.

Gray swirls of mist blanketed the valley, and Miles's heart sank. He would have been better off simply following the path after all.

Still, he refused to succumb to sentimental lamentations, and he stared longer at the mist, willing it to shift. The fog moved, but no rider was revealed. He gritted his teeth.

Five minutes. He'd wait five minutes longer.

The horse still whinnied, stomping its hooves into the muddy path, perhaps enraged that its Arabic ancestors had managed to sire offspring stuck in so cold and dismal a region.

Miles had almost decided to turn around, when he saw a horse and rider trot underneath one of the gaps in the mist.

Veronique.

He was certain.

She wore a dark cape and had somehow managed to ride astride, but her figure was too slender to belong to a man, and the sides of her dark dress billowed in the wind. She leaned her back forward, as if seeking to meld with her horse.

, she was beautiful, even riding one hundred feet below him.

There was another, thinner line etched into the valley, and Miles wondered if it was a second road. It joined the path she traveled on later. If he could take that path and blockade the road she was taking—he grinned.

He'd find her. He was certain of it.

He beamed, happy for the first time this morning.

He returned to his horse, and it galloped past supine sheep, unconcerned with the stone and mud. Nature's attempts at barriers failed to daunt the beast, and Miles relaxed into the saddle.

His brother, Marcus, was right to adore this region. He and his wife Rosamund enjoyed rambling, and academics lauded Marcus's opuses on the natural world.

Science never held the same sway for Miles, despite his appreciation for fresh air and pleasingly formed plants. Recording the life cycle of shrubs could not compete with recording the curtailment of human life. Instead he'd spread stories of Bonaparte's cruelty and insatiable craving for power.

Miles had interviewed British soldiers in makeshift hospitals tasked with halting Bonaparte, as other men howled when the surgeon sawed off their ill-functioning limbs, and others had succumbed to fevers, spending their final days in an incessant swirl of scorching heat and icy cold that only they felt.

Miles had wandered the battlefields, trudging over red smeared snow. He'd visited Italian and Austrian towns, the stone buildings toppled, as bewildered peasants had sobbed.

British citizens should clamor at the government when a battle went awry. The stakes, not only for British soldiers, but for Britain and the world itself, could not be ignored.

When an army contractor allotted defective shoes to British soldiers, Miles had reported on soldiers sliding to their deaths, and of the heightened frequency of frostbite indicated with the sudden prevalence of surgeons chopping off toes.

Once he caught up with Veronique, he would concentrate on his search for Loretta Van Lochen. Making increasingly awkward conversations with his newly given to romanticism brothers lacked appeal.

He sighed. Reporting on Loretta Van Lochen in no manner rivaled those stories in importance. Love was a fairytale for most, and he had no sympathies for a woman who profited on the proliferation of those fantasies. Women would be far better served with fighting for equal education than whiling away their time reading of imaginary princes battling still more imaginary villains. In his experience, royals seemed the least likely to do any true fighting, and there were many real problems in this world to focus on.

The sun swathed the path in light.

By now the servants must have discovered Veronique and him missing from their bed chambers. Had they roused his brothers? Would they be searching for him? Or would they assume he'd simply helped himself to a horse for an early morning jaunt, and Veronique had vanished for a similarly explicable reason?

She'd been clever to flee the castle at dawn. Most of the *ton* didn't rouse until far later, and in such a massive castle, it would take a while to determine they were missing at all, particularly if the servants were of the discreet variety and did not panic at the sight of an empty bed.

They reached the smaller road, and Miles urged his horse forward. Perhaps the narrow width rendered the road impassible in summer, but absurd amounts of leaves and thorns did not yet burst from the brambles.

Soon he would overtake Veronique. Would she stop when she saw him? Or would she see his form only as indication that she should galvanize her horse to a gallop?

What he needed was some impediment to ensure she halt. Hadn't the Duke and Duchess of Alfriston met because his coach had stopped for a fallen tree? All he had to do was take out his knife, cut down some threatening looking branches, and he would be sweeping Veronique back to the castle in no time. He beamed, eager to see the expression on her face.

"Whoa," he murmured to the horse, and it halted. He stepped onto the soft soil and started to fasten the reins to a tree.

He required something to inspire Veronique to slow her horse. Farmers or poachers likely already had some good traps. Perhaps a net was nearby? He gazed up at the tree, willing himself to find something, anything, which might halt her relentless march toward London.

She would be appearing soon.

Of course no net was to be found, and he sighed and continued to tie the reins to the tree. He moved back to tighten his knot, and then he—

Fell.

It took him a second to identify the action. The plunge knocked the breath from his lungs, and he plummeted downward.

In the next moment mud squished beneath him, and dried twigs and leaves snapped and crunched in a cacophony of protest.

Blast.

Miles scrambled up.

Or at least—he attempted to scramble up.

The task of standing had never demanded much attention, but it now seemed to rank as one of the most difficult tasks in the world.

His left ankle quaked beneath him, and pain shot through his body.

Double blast.

He inched his way up, clinging onto the slippery mud walls.

His clothes were stained, and his always perfectly coiffed hair, a testament to his valet, must appear in a revolting state. He lifted his arms toward the ledge.

I can't reach it.

I'm stuck.

His heart toppled downward, and he shivered. How on earth had he found himself trapped in a hole in the middle of the Scottish Highlands?

Perhaps the farmer or poacher who formed the hole

would come check on it—but how long would such a wait be? He was cold, blast it.

The sky was still above him, though the dark gray shade, present on every of the few occasions he'd allowed his brother to drag him to Scotland, was hardly enticing.

He swallowed hard. What were the chances it might rain?

This was Scotland, so the chances were significantly higher that it would rain than it would not.

He cursed the fact he'd ever attempted to go after Veronique.

A rustling sounded, and he turned his head toward the horse

The horse that was moving away from him.

He narrowed his eyes, as if the act of contracting his eyelids might right the appalling view.

Though squeezing his eyelids together did manage to make the sight look less drastic, it did not hinder the horse from ambling away.

"Whoa," he called.

He was good with horses. The horse would stop.

The horse did not stop.

"Whoa," he called again, this time increasing his volume.

He wasn't certain if he'd managed to keep his voice from shaking. Perhaps it was just as well that Scotland was less populated than Mayfair, and no members of the *ton* would witness his distress.

Unfortunately no members of the *ton* would be present to rescue him.

He shook his head. That was nonsense. He was in no need of rescuing. In fact, he was here to rescue somebody. Quite a different manner entirely.

The horse reached its previous speed and galloped toward the castle.

Well.

Miles scowled.

He hadn't liked the length of the journey from the castle, and that had been when he'd been sitting on somebody doing the walking. Now he was trapped in some beastly hole like a blasted deer.

Damnation.

His ankle ached. Perhaps the cold would distract him from the pain.

If only he had some sort of beacon—not that the passersby swarmed this place.

Though he'd wandered off the main road, and Veronique unlikely traveled through bushes when a perfectly fine path was available, she remained his best hope.

Perhaps my only hope.

Chapter Nine

The dark gray sky lifted, replacing the somber clouds with a more traditional celestial image. It might not be the azure sweeps of color found in her reference books to Italy and Spain, but the occasional glimpses of actual blue more than satisfied her.

The few leaves glimmered under the sun, and squirrels and chipmunks pattered over branches, as if attempting to race Graeme and her.

Some grass clung to the dark mud, and she closed her eyes, envisioning the seeds strewn over the earth and the blossoms and buds that would soon force their way to the surface.

Life was good.

And soon it will be marvelous.

Something white flickered in the distance. A stocking? She frowned.

Was this something that belonged to some peasant? Had some man been so overtaken by the degree-climb of the temperature, that he'd stripped off a single stocking in glee?

Even Scotsmen didn't seem that absurd.

She frowned.

Perhaps a village was nearby.

She looked around, but only trees and bushes confronted her.

A noise sounded.

A noise that sounded very much like...shouting.

She shivered.

Some birds still chirped merrily, as if incognizant at the yammering that had joined their chorus.

She slowed her horse.

A deep voice sounded. A man was definitely shouting.

And people consider Americans eccentric.

She wavered, unsure whether to head straight past or investigate.

She gazed into the clearing, but besides the white stockings, she couldn't see anyone.

"Is someone there?" Her voice wobbled, and she winced. Of course someone was there. Perhaps one of the returned soldiers rumored to wander the country looking for a work they never found.

"Help!" a voice shouted. "I'm stuck."

She narrowed her gaze. The man certainly did not sound like a wayward peasant or soldier. He didn't even sound Scottish.

His accent had the rounded vowels that made her think of someone else entirely.

She shook her head. She shouldn't be thinking about Lord Worthing, no matter how pleasant their kiss.

Naturally it wouldn't be that man—they were far from anyone in the middle of nowhere. She'd snuck from the castle early in the morning. Lord Worthing was likely having tea and crumpets with her family now in the centuries-old dining room. Perhaps they were pondering her propensity to oversleep.

She retained a firm hold on Graeme's reins in case urging him to a gallop proved necessary. "Where are you?"

"I'm in a blasted hole!" The man sputtered indignantly, and Veronique's lips twitched.

Veronique slid from her horse, tied it to a nearby tree and inched toward the sound.

And then she saw the hole.

"One moment." She crept forward slowly, lest there be more holes in this region.

She peeked her head over the hole—and paused.

A very muddy Lord Worthing scowled at her.

"What are you doing here?"

"I could ask the same of you." He crossed his arms and gave her a lofty frown not suited to his position.

"I'm not sitting in filth," she said.

"Well…" He paused. "That was unintentional."

"Were you searching for me?" She tilted her head, not bothering to keep the suspicion from her voice. "How many more of you are there?"

She glanced around, half-expecting to see Lord Worthing's strapping brothers clamber from trees and pop up from boulders.

"It's just me," he said mournfully.

"And I should believe that?"

"Because I damned don't like sitting in holes. It's dirty here."

His indignation didn't seem feigned, and she smiled.

"My valet is going to murder me when I return to England," Lord Worthing continued.

"Perhaps I should make it easier for him and leave you here."

"N-no." Lord Worthing attempted to scramble up, and then groaned loudly.

"You hurt your ankle."

"I did," the man grumbled. "And now I'm stuck."

"Oh, dear."

"Please fetch help from the castle," Lord Worthing demanded.

She frowned. "Never."

"But my ankle—" Lord Worthing huffed. "I need help. You can get my brothers or some servants."

"Nonsense. I can't turn back," she said firmly. "I'm on a mission to see the love of my life. I won't permit anybody to stop me."

Lord Worthing blinked. "You really mean that?"

"Naturally."

"But..." he hesitated, but then barreled on, "...he left you. At the altar."

Veronique cringed, but she pushed her misgivings aside. "One day we will laugh at it, I'm sure."

"He's not acting like a man in love."

She stiffened and looked away. "I know he loves me. There was a reason, I'm certain."

"You are too romantic."

She tossed her hair. "I have a wonderful connection with him. He is the most brilliant man who's ever lived."

"So you won't get somebody to haul me out of this..."

Veronique smiled. "No. I'm going to rescue you."

He blinked. "That's good." He paused. "I don't like to draw attention to my size, but I'm far heavier than you. All these muscles, after all." He smirked, and she rolled her eyes.

*

Miles's ankle throbbed as Veronique peered at the slippery muddy walls of his new abode.

"How did you land here?" she asked.

"I was attempting to rescue you," he grumbled. "I saw you from my window. Those bedsheets could have torn," he said sternly.

"At least I used bedsheets." Veronique smiled most maddeningly. "I saw someone scale down the castle wall. I assume that was you?"

Pride flickered through him. "Indeed."

"I wasn't certain given your current predicament at a much shorter challenge."

"The pit was obscured." He scowled and gestured at the leaves and branches that had fallen with him.

"Hmph."

"This is a crisis," he reminded her.

She gazed about her. Perhaps for a miracle. "Did you walk here?"

Warmth crept up his cheeks, and he directed his gaze to the compilation of dried leaves and gnarly twigs. Anything to escape the inevitable mirth in her eyes. "My horse ran away."

"Your reputation as a horse rider did not include the inability to retain a horse."

He shrugged. "The horse had a proper distaste for Scottish roads. One you should possess."

"Evidently the horse is not in love." Veronique sighed. "Do you have a knife? Men tend to carry weapons."

He fumbled with his boot and removed the knife he always kept there for emergencies. "You know too much about men."

"I make it my business to know about them." This time

her smile was almost mysterious, and he had to resist the urge to gaze into her eyes, like some dewy-eyed lad fresh from Eton at his first ball.

He handed her his knife. "If you leave me, I'll have nothing to defend myself with against wild animals."

"I'll keep that in mind," she called out and disappeared.

His heartbeat thumped in protest.

Surely she wouldn't...abandon him?

Damnation.

His heartbeat scuttled, and he attempted again to hoist himself from the hole. Though his arms were strong, they were not of sufficiently long length to grip the hole's ledge. He slid back into the pit, his hands more muddied.

Next time he saw a damsel in distress, he would do the correct thing: close his curtains and slip back underneath his warm covers.

After a few agonizing minutes, Veronique appeared and slid a long branch down.

Dried leaves toppled into the hole, and Miles narrowed his eyes.

"Climb onto this," Veronique said in a matter-of-fact tone a hostess might best use when directing someone to her drawing room.

She seemed oblivious to the fact that branches were not normal transport.

"It will never work," he grumbled.

"Just try it."

He frowned. Obviously the chit overestimated his toleration for blisters, but when he came closer, he realized she'd carved grips into the thick branch so it functioned similarly to a ladder.

"Stick the end in the mud so it has a good foundation," she ordered.

He did so and tentatively stepped onto it.

The branch did not fall or crumble beneath his feet.

His ankle still quaked with pain as he put his weight over it, but he could do this. He'd been through worse. Nothing would ever compare to that burst of terror when he'd spotted French cavalry galloping toward him on the battlefield, lances drawn to impale everything in sight.

He hoisted himself up and flung himself onto the ground. The feel of thick tree roots beneath his hands was the most blissful sensation in the world.

"Your ankle hurts?"

"I'm fine." He grunted and attempted to look slightly less relieved.

No way was he going to let Veronique think him vulnerable. It might make her more liable to fleeing. Or...laughing at him.

"Let me bandage it for you."

"It's not bleeding."

"It will benefit from having some cloth bound tightly around it. No point having it take weeks to heal."

"How do you know all that?"

She smiled mysteriously again. "Do as I say."

He remained suspicious, but perhaps arguing with a woman who grasped his knife lacked wisdom.

He reached for the stocking, but pain fired through him. "Bloody hell."

"Allow me," Veronique said.

Miles scowled. Women were supposed to marvel at the muscularity of his limbs, admiring their firmness, visible even through tailcoats. They should yearn for him to guide them over the ballroom floor, and they should flush in pleasure if he offered them his arm. They definitely were not supposed to gaze at him as if they'd mistaken him for an injured puppy. It was not conducive to the maintenance of a healthy self-image.

Veronique touched his ankle, and he abhorred the way his body shivered under her touch, as if the furthest extremities of his body had memorized the way she'd made him feel yesterday.

Her face seemed to pale, but she soon wrapped his stocking efficiently about him. "Can you walk?"

"Naturally!" He was affronted. "I climbed that makeshift ladder."

"And I've never seen a face so white," she said.

"I can walk," he repeated, but he glanced at the branch. "Perhaps I should have a walking stick. And then we can return to the castle."

"Oh, no," she said. "I'm going to London."

"Not Austria?"

Her eyes widened. "That would be absurd."

"London is absurd..."

"He works in London." Veronique's eyes shone. "He's a diplomat."

"It's not proper to go alone—"

She shrugged. "Now I have a companion."

Blast.

"A young man of marriageable age does not meet the basic qualifications of a companion," he reminded her.

"Do you often mull over how you're of 'marriageable age'?" Veronique's tone might be innocent, but the sparkle of her eyes and swift upward sweep of her lips were not.

Miles glowered, but somehow the action simply made her lips glide further up. He gazed away. Mulling over her lips might lead to thoughts of touching her lips. And that, blast it, might lead to *remembering* the taste of her lips.

"We were already discovered in a compromising position, and if we return to the castle, we'll be forced to wed," Veronique said.

"Right." Miles croaked.

"Once I find my baron, I can marry him, and you will be freed from my father's and stepmother's urgings to be honorable toward me." She tossed her hair, and he withdrew his gaze from her.

The urge to contemplate her curly locks, and the way the few sunbeams managed to play in her hair, was overly tempting.

"Fine." He scowled and eyed her horse. It was hardly a racing horse. "You may have an unduly small image of Britain. We might be small compared to America, but it still takes a long time to traverse. That horse won't make it."

"Oh, I know. There's an inn near here where coaches stop. I stole a map." She grinned. "We can catch the mail coach toward London. You owe me."

Miles attempted to glare at her. "I would have managed."

"Ha." She brushed off more dirt that clung to her gown. "Unlikely."

"The trap was not obvious," Miles grumbled.

"They seldom are." Veronique's eyes gleamed. "But perhaps you can write to Scotland and suggest they create better sign postings."

Miles frowned. "So who is this German baron?"

"He's Austrian. And more wonderful than you could ever imagine." Veronique tossed her hair, and Miles regretted that he'd chosen just that topic to switch the conversation to.

"I'm sure he doesn't go about hiding in holes so he can accompany women," Veronique continued.

"I was trying to save you," Miles huffed.

"And yet I was the person doing the saving," Veronique mused.

"I suppose I should have bloody let you venture out on your own."

She frowned. "You shouldn't curse."

"This is precisely the sort of occasion that demands cursing, Veronica."

"It's Veronique," she said, and something about the indignant way she wrinkled her nose was almost charming.

In fact far too many things about her were charming.

Chapter Ten

The pained expression on Lord Worthing's face had not dissipated.

"Let's get you on the horse," Veronique said.

No need to linger on their assured lateness. The sun would set whatever they did, and they better be at an inn. Veronique had no desire to spend the night underneath the stars with Lord Worthing. Not when her nerve endings still didn't seem to realize that the man was the incorrect baron.

Lord Worthing frowned. "On your horse?"

"You're in no suitable condition to walk even a short distance." She hesitated, bracing for the man's scowl to strengthen. He did seem to be imbued with a large degree of masculinity and a propensity to defend it.

Instead he simply nodded. "Very well."

Veronique blinked.

And then dread surged through her.

Did he intend to return to the castle after all? Gallop away at full force and lead a search party of strapping Scottish servants to haul her away?

"I'll of course join you," she said quickly.

He scrutinized her. Somehow everything seemed easier when he was not directing the full force of his eyes toward her.

"On the horse," she said. "I'll ride with you."

"Indeed?"

For some reason his voice was hoarse.

Perhaps he'd developed a cold from sitting in the pit, and Veronique softened her gaze. "The horse is strong."

Lord Worthing nodded and clambered onto the horse, hauling his bad ankle behind him.

"Should I sit in the front?" she asked.

"Behind is better," he said, his voice still strained.

She nodded and moved toward Graeme. She placed her toe in the stirrup, and Lord Worthing leaned forward and swept her onto the horse.

"Th-thank you."

"My arms are fully functioning," he said.

Even though the distance from the ground to the top of the horse in no manner rivaled a mountain, her heartbeat still quickened, and she strove to steady her breath, as if she'd just climbed the Matterhorn.

"You'll need to sit closer to me," Lord Worthing said. "The horse is not massive in size."

"Right." Her fingers trembled, but she slid her legs beside Lord Worthing's so that her pantalettes touched his trousers. Riding astride was indecent. "Like this?"

Her voice sounded more high-pitched than normal. The man shouldn't smell so good after lying in a hole for heavens knew how long, but her nostrils still flared, inhaling the masculine mixture of cotton and sweat.

"Grab hold of my waist," he directed her. "I can't have you toppling down too."

"Very well." Her voice seemed to have decided to settle on a higher octave than normal, and she decided that talking might not be a requirement.

Lord Worthing urged the horse to a trot, and she attempted to focus on the shifting scenery and not on the muscular length of his back and the way his dark locks curled behind his ears, as if urging someone to touch it.

She needed something, anything else to focus on.

"Would you like some food?" She fumbled in her satchel and handed him a cold meat pie.

"I suppose I shouldn't ask where you got this."

"You might not like the answer." She smiled, remembering sneaking into the kitchen late at night.

He chuckled. "In other words I'm helping my brother's thief make an escape?"

She laughed.

"You should be happy Lord Rockport was my older brother. I might feel more protective of him otherwise."

"I'm sure his cook will be able to make more meat pies for him."

"Well... Thank you." Lord Worthing gobbled the pie so gratefully that guilt shot through her.

He hadn't planned to follow her. Hadn't even wanted to. And yet he'd risked his life to do so.

If he'd fallen while scaling the castle wall... If she hadn't come across him now... She swallowed hard.

"I was impressed that you'd climbed down the wall," she admitted.

"Ah... If only you had stayed to praise me then." Lord Worthing's voice was warm, as if he were smiling.

"Where did you learn to do that? I'm sure that wasn't on your curriculum at Eton."

He laughed. "How did you know I went to Eton?"

"Most men of your class go there."

"Some go to Rugby or Harrow, but you're correct...Eton is the best. The uniforms are the most dashing."

"Perhaps to make up for the fact that their graduates while about in muddied attire."

"That was an accident," Lord Worthing said sternly, and she giggled.

"Now," Lord Worthing spoke between bites into his meat pie, "I am afraid you may have an overly optimistic impression of the size of Britain. Just because we are an island does not mean we are tiny."

"Naturally."

"It will take a while to get to London. A very long while. This horse will not be able to carry both of us there."

"I've planned for everything," Veronique said.

"What about accommodation?"

"There's an inn in the next village."

"Indeed?" Lord Worthing snapped a dry branch back to make room for her, and she resisted the urge to lean against his broad back.

"The mail coach stops there," Veronique said. "We'll be able to get a coach that goes in the direction of London."

"Would that be at *The Red Hart*?"

"You know it?"

"I was there yesterday. Before we...met."

"Oh." Veronique's heartbeat may have quickened. Their meeting had been rather memorable.

She slid back further, as if a mere centimeter might make her possibly forget the taste of his lips, and the feel of his strong arms.

"It would be quicker if we crossed through this farmer's field," Lord Worthing said authoritatively.

Veronique hesitated. Reaching the inn earlier held a definite temptation.

She shook her head. "I think we should abide to the path."

Lord Worthing shrugged. "If you enjoy my company so much..."

She despised the smug smirk in his voice. She was betrothed.

She frowned. "Very well. If you're absolutely certain."

"Of course." The horse plodded through the trees away from the main path and onto a field. A few cows scrutinized them with seeming skepticism, and the horse's clomps quieted against the softer soil, freed from fallen twigs and branches.

"Your baron should have been here himself."

"Perhaps he was facing a crisis."

"Such as a personal crisis?"

Veronique despised the amusement in Lord Worthing's tone. "You're fortunate I'm behind you."

"Oh?"

"Because I'm glaring very hard."

He laughed. "Then that's the first bit of fortune I've had today."

Veronique refused to join his laughter, no matter how warm it sounded. She tossed her hair. "He's likely facing a European crisis."

"The war's over, Miss Daventry."

"He's a diplomat. He's likely preventing all sorts of wars from happening."

"How heroic of him," Lord Worthing said, and Veronique despised that the humor hadn't left his voice.

"You wouldn't understand the great work he does."

"Please do tell why you believe that."

"You're just a rogue. You don't do anything."

"That's not true," Lord Worthing said.

"Well. I suppose you might count going to parties, to gentlemen's clubs, or kissing women when you first meet them—"

Perhaps it had been wrong to bring up the kissing. Her blood seemed to rush through her body despite her best wishes.

"Is that all my brothers have told you?" The humor in his voice had vanished, but Veronique continued. Somehow arguing with him seemed less dangerous than laughing with him.

"Was there anything more?"

"Yes, there was." He sighed. "I suppose it doesn't matter."

"Well, do tell me," she said finally. "It's not like we're exactly short on time."

"It's not important. At least...not anymore," he said.

She was beginning to understand. The war had been massive. There had been so many people who'd joined the army and the navy. Guilt rippled through her. "Were you a soldier?"

Her sister's husband, the Duke of Belmonte, had been a sailor in the navy for years. When the war had ended, he had not come back, unable to conceive of his life in England.

She'd never had that issue. The past had never been pleasant enough to stop hoping for the future. The future had always been her preferred place to be, if not her future, then the future of the people in stories.

"I wasn't a soldier," he said finally. "I could have been. I would have been wonderful at it."

"I'm sure," she said genuinely.

"I was a foreign correspondent."

She blinked. "There weren't many of those."

"No," he said, and his voice once again sounded warm. "There weren't."

"So what exactly does a foreign correspondent do?" she asked.

"Report on international news." He shrugged. "Most newspapers belong to a single party. They're either Whig or Tory. Obviously you can get very biased news that way. There's little point buying a newspaper if you always know what it's going to say. Some broadsheets always supported the government, others never did."

"I see," she said.

"My publisher sent me overseas so that I could get the real news, not obtained from government propaganda, or the often equally false propaganda created by the other side. They sent me to Spain, Austria, Italy—everywhere Bonaparte went, I followed."

Oh.

Perhaps he hadn't been a diplomat, but he'd certainly helped his country.

"Wasn't that dangerous?"

He shrugged. "War is dangerous."

"But you weren't even a soldier. You didn't have even the advantage of ranks of people with guns fighting beside you. There weren't cavalry backing you up."

"I survived. Got some damn good articles out of it too."

"How did you become a foreign correspondent?"

"I always liked writing."

Veronique nodded. She understood that.

"And I was good at languages at school. I spoke French and German. Latin and Greek were rather less helpful, only allowing me to read the letters on the ancient buildings in Rome."

"Rome! How wonderful."

"It was rather."

"I would love to visit one day," Veronique mused.

"Perhaps Lord Braunschweig will take you," he said. "It's easy to go overseas now that the French aren't firing at all the ships on the English Channel that haven't donned the French flag. It's still a bit unpleasant to travel, but I suspect you're up for it."

She grinned back, and for some reason warmth rushed through her. "I would love to convince Lord Braunschweig to do that."

"You think that might be difficult?"

"I suppose not. He's a diplomat. Traveling and moving is something to be expected. But he's always made it quite clear that England is the best place in the world to be. I should be content just being here. It is nicer than the other countries. It is nice to be in a land where slavery is forbidden," she added more softly.

"But surely England isn't the absolute best," he said. "France has excellent cheese, and Bonaparte gathered all the most impressive paintings together before he was deposed."

"Oh, I heard about that."

"You're rather well read for an American."

"I have the time. At least I've had access to reading material," Veronique said, thinking of all the time she'd been confined to her room. No need to mull over that. "What brings you to Scotland? Fraternal affection? I'm sorry I dragged you away."

"Don't worry," Lord Worthing said. "I'll see Gerard again. Ever since he and his wife married, he's been to London more and more often. I see enough of him at the big balls there."

"I see. Good."

"Actually I'm here on an assignment," Lord Worthing said. "One I'm not doing. I'll have a bloody angry publisher after me now. I was hoping to go back overseas, but it might be difficult when I don't do this one investigative piece for him."

"In Scotland? In the Highlands? What is there possibly for you to investigate here? Sheep and cow movement?"

"That's quite an interesting thing," he said. "More Scots are fleeing to Canada and America."

"Indeed."

"But I shouldn't tell you about my assignment."

"Oh, please," Veronique said. "I would be so delighted."

"I really shouldn't. You can read about it later."

"Maybe I can give you guidance. Since I've been here longer. Is it a jewel thief perhaps? Murderer?"

He laughed. "The scariest thing here are the farmers, and that's only for the sheep to concern themselves with. Promise you won't tell anyone."

"Now who could I possibly tell? Besides, I'm good at keeping secrets." She smirked.

"It's Loretta Van Lochen."

Fear surged through her.

What on earth was this about? Was this the reason he'd followed her outside? Did he know who she was? Was this all some fluff piece?

Her publisher had warned her to remain anonymous. One thing was to publish books from an author who was descended from slaves, but quite another was to attempt to sell it when all the readers knew about the person's questionable heritage.

"L-Loretta Van Lochen. Who is that?" she asked carefully.

"I'm surprised you don't know who she is, given her popularity."

"I favor the anonymous author of *Sense and Sensibility* more myself." She raked a hand through her hair and tried to appear innocent.

"Oh, you're one of those women," he said.

"What is that supposed to mean?"

"Never mind. I suppose you do show some taste."

Veronique's hands tightened about his waist.

"Loretta Van Lochen writes the most absurd books," Lord Worthing continued. "Ridiculous storylines. All about princesses in towers and handsome heroes who rescue them. Utter nonsense."

"I suppose you've tried reading her?"

"Oh, yes. Merely for research purposes. Quite nonsensical."

"Indeed?" She strove to keep her voice calm. Outrage was perhaps not the emotion she wanted to convey. "Why would Loretta Van Lochen be here? Is she Scottish?"

He shrugged. "Part of her mystery. She started writing a few years ago. All we know is that the name is a pen name. No, no one knows who she is."

"And why would she be here?"

"She wrote three books in a row set in Scotland."

"A coincidence," Veronique said icily.

"That's what I think," Lord Worthing said.

"How curious."

"Well not that curious," Lord Worthing said. "Who

cares about this woman? But now I'm forced to investigate such banality, using all the skills I honed in the war."

Veronique tensed. "And now I'm not letting you do that."

He shrugged.

"How horrible," she said, attempting to laugh, but conscious the sound seemed unconvincing. She was spending time with the one person she absolutely shouldn't.

"Your safety is more important." He nodded firmly. "I won't leave your side."

Chapter Eleven

The light shifted as the horse trudged through the fields. Dark shadows pervaded the ever-darkening lane. Miles's ankle continued to throb, and he endeavored to ignore that he'd just traveled up all the way from the English Channel to turn around.

"Are you certain there is an inn here?" Veronique asked.

"Naturally."

At least, he'd been certain.

He'd visited it yesterday, for goodness' sake.

But perhaps he'd been mistaken after all.

Raindrops fell.

"Merely some Scottish sprinkles." Miles forced his voice to sound light. "Good for the horse."

"Hmph."

At least the rain did not seem very hard.

Yet.

If this was what passed as good conversation in Massachusetts, he was dashed glad George III had not put up a better fight for the colonies.

Miles sighed.

Ever since he'd declared his assignment to discover the whereabouts of Loretta Van Lochen, she'd been quiet. It was all too clear that she'd been horrified by the banality of his task.

Clearly he contrasted poorly to the correct baron, and Miles scowled. There'd been a time when people had lauded him for his work.

He tried to discern the outline of an inn. He would gladly accept even an older inn. Even somebody's house.

Everything was dark, and the few faint forms were those of trees.

The rain continued to dapple on them, growing in force.

And then he saw it.

Miles braced to discover some strange Gaelic rock grouping instead of an accommodation option, but as they neared, moonlight revealed the most delightful thing.

It was not, he was certain, an inn. At least it couldn't be the same posting inn he'd stopped at on the way to his brother. This building lacked *The Red Hart's* even mediocre dimensions, and the walls sloped inward in such a manner that *The Red Hart* seemed a paragon of construction prowess, one bright-eyed architecture students in Edinburgh could study when they tired of continental cathedrals.

He maneuvered the horse toward the building. "Splendid."

Miles hobbled from the horse, cursing his still aching ankle.

"It's a barn," Veronique gasped.

"Yes," he said happily, sliding open the door. "With a roof and everything."

He led the horse into the barn. "No need for it to sleep outside. We can all be together."

"I can't spend the night alone with you," Veronique said. "That would be improper."

Miles yawned. "You left propriety at the castle."

"If anyone learns of this—"

"They'll want me to marry you." He shrugged. "Follow me."

Miles fumbled until he found a lantern. He lit a much-melted candle and illuminated the hay loft and exposed timber beams. "This is the accommodation to expect when one runs away."

"And when one listens to barons who lack a proper directional sense," Veronique murmured.

Miles cleared his throat. "My ankle might not be at the peak of its form, but I assure you that my ears are fully functioning."

"I rather expected that," Veronique said.

"Hmph." Miles focused on exploring their new dwelling. Straw was scattered on the ground with such abundance, he wondered whether it was the result of carelessness or some replacement of an actual floor.

"The thing is—" Miles strode toward her and vowed not to be distracted by the gold flecks that danced in her eyes. This was important. "You mustn't forget that I absolutely do not want to marry you."

She flinched.

Pink stormed her cheeks, and she tilted her head toward the stalls. "I should feed Graeme."

She moved briskly away, led the horse into an empty stall, and found food and water for it.

Her head might be inclined from him, but the tension

in her shoulders and the way her fingers curled together could not be disguised.

The joy he thought he would receive from assuring her of his disinterest failed to arrive.

He'd gone too far.

Guilt surged through him.

Veronique had just had one man jilt her. She might be clinging to the hope that her fiancé had experienced a mishap, rather than a reassessment of his marital goals, but that didn't mean Miles should insult her. Even the most stubborn woman might experience some insecurity at the sight of an empty altar.

He raked a hand through his hair and settled on a wooden bench. It creaked underneath his weight, seeming to echo through the barn but she did not turn toward him.

At least he'd been honest. His childhood tutors had extolled the quality.

But a strange feeling prickled through him, a sense his statement hadn't been entirely honest.

Because yesterday afternoon had been bloody brilliant. He'd never had a kiss so good.

He shook his head. It didn't matter what he'd thought of her yesterday. She'd already made her disinterest toward him clear. "Let's sleep."

He pointed toward the hayloft. "This will be the warmest place."

"Then you go there," she said sternly.

"But—"

"I was born in Barbados. I spent enough of my life getting warm. I'm sure I'll manage without an elevated temperature for a night."

"It wouldn't be gentlemanly of me to permit—"

She waved her hand at him in a dismissive manner.

"You've insulted me enough. I'm certain you can be ungentlemanly when I request it."

He inhaled.

Her expression was defiant. Fire seemed to gleam through her eyes, and she raised her chin.

The woman had a point.

"Very well," he said finally and hauled himself up the ladder, using his arms more than the task normally required to best alleviate the pressure on his ankle.

*

Wind whistled through cracks in the wooden wall. Perhaps Veronique had been outside all day, but now she was no longer moving, no longer occupying her mind with avoiding bristly bushes and gnarly tree roots, and certainly no longer defending herself from the baron, tiredness swept over her.

She shivered.

"I have something for you." Lord Worthing's voice boomed from above, and she gazed up.

He smiled at her and raised a tartan blanket triumphantly. "We're not the only ones who've slept here before. Catch!"

The woolen blanket floated down to her, and she grabbed the coarse fabric gladly. It seemed clean, at least in comparison to the rest of the barn, and she swept it around her shoulders.

Lord Worthing's eyes seemed to soften, but he soon turned away.

She wrapped the blanket more tightly about her.

"Plenty of hay too," he called out.

Something sounded from above, and then a stack of

hay thudded onto the ground. Some of the horses gave startled neighs, but Veronique smiled. "Thank you."

She pushed the hay into a corner and settled onto her makeshift bed.

Just a few days more.

And then she would see the baron, the true one, and all would be well.

The candlelight flickered, nearly extinguished, and she removed some pages from her satchel. She ran her fingers over the swooping swirls.

The familiar letters, the words long memorized, calmed her, and she reread the letter until the candle extinguished and she fell asleep.

Chapter Twelve

G ruff voices murmured outside, and Veronique
scrambled up. Hay prickled her palms, and she slid
from her makeshift bed as her heart lurched.

People were speaking, might be entering the barn,
and—

Veronique had no desire to contemplate the
consequences of discovery. Likely breaking and entering
was no more tolerated in Scotland than America.

The voices strengthened and heavy footsteps plodded
outside.

Goodness.

Veronique's heart lurched unevenly inside her chest,
and she flung the blanket around her shoulders and
rushed up the ladder. She crawled over the loft, the coarse
straw insufficient protection against the rough
floorboards.

Something sounded, and she recognized the rhythmic
breathing of someone sleeping.

The door slid open, and men tramped inside.

Somebody fumbled near the entrance, and she drew in her breath. Likely they were searching for the light.

Perhaps rereading love letters last night had lacked necessity.

"Ye shouldn't move the lantern," one man grumbled. "Everything has a place. That's what me mum always said."

"I didna move it," the other person complained.

More rustling sounded.

Lord Worthing stirred, and her breath quickened. Was he waking up? Would he...say anything?

She eased down beside him, as if the ratcheting of her heartbeat might disturb the people below.

The farmers continued to grumble.

Her heart sped; they would discover the horse. Counting was not an ability limited to mathematicians.

Lord Worthing yawned.

Fiddlesticks.

He was awake.

He stirred on his hay stack groggily, and she had a moment of sympathy for him. This wasn't a good situation. No one should wake to it.

"That horse wasn't there last night," one of the farmers mulled. His voice boomed through the room, the placement of the barn's rafters heightening its natural strength.

Lord Worthing stirred again and started to murmur.

Veronique didn't think.

She placed her hand over his mouth, trying not to note the softness of his lips and the masculine roughness of his stubble.

He squirmed, and she ducked her face down.

Dim light from the lantern below illuminated the chiseled angles of his face, roughened with stubble.

His eyes widened and then relaxed, as if her presence might be a source of calm.

She pointed in the direction of the voices, and his face firmed.

"You don't suppose there's anyone here?" one farmer asked, and the light flickered toward them.

Lord Worthing's jaw steadied, and he yanked her toward him.

She blinked.

She was lying on top of a...man.

She'd never done something so scandalous in her life.

Her face reddened, as she remembered she had in fact done something more scandalous. They'd kissed. The experience had been so blissful, so utterly wonderful—and so forbidden.

She was engaged to someone else.

But thoughts of the baron's letters failed to draw her attention away from the warm body beneath her.

The farmers continued to murmur, and Lord Worthing tightened his grip around her.

He didn't need to do so.

Nothing would compel her to leave, not when strange men might discover their intrusion. .

Would they be scolded? Or hauled to the magistrate?

She refused to allow the latter to become a possibility and refrained from the inclination to squeal.

Lord Worthing's eyes flickered with something like concern, and she relaxed against his broad chest, conscious of the outline of his muscles.

His arms shouldn't feel so sturdy around her waist, and

she railed against the absurd urge to trace them with her fingers.

She was an engaged woman. Soon she would marry a man she didn't need to meet to know was wonderful.

Yet the achingly narrow distance between Lord Worthing and herself seemed of far more interest than the men below.

His hands tapped against her, likely to comfort her against the uncertainty of the farmers discovering them, but the gesture only caused her heart to gallop.

It was too easy to remember his lips on hers, too easy to remember the joy she'd experienced at their meeting. She'd attempted to push away the unease she'd had ever since she planned to elope, but when she first met him in that chapel, when she'd believed him to be her fiancé, he'd shattered all her doubts.

She swallowed hard.

Lord Worthing remained a practical stranger, someone who accompanied her only out of a desire to avoid marriage with her. He'd stated the fact himself. He was not her husband-to-be.

He was not even a friend.

*

Being roused by a pretty woman was normally to be celebrated, but Miles despised the worry that seeped through Veronique.

He did his best to reassure her, brushing his fingers against her back, even as the men sounded below.

The farmers directed their attention to grumbling about the weather, a no doubt endless endeavor in this rain subjected land.

Finally the door slammed shut, and the voices stopped. *We're alone.*

Miles shouldn't desire to pull Veronique toward him. But when she raised her torso, something like disappointment surged through him.

He shook his head.

The men's absence was good.

Veronique and he could start going about their day. *Perfect.*

She climbed from him and brushed hay from her dress. "We should go," Veronique said finally.

"Yes."

He rose from his makeshift bed and hastened down the ladder, ignoring the twinges of pain that shot through him with his every move.

Veronique followed him from the barn. "But the horse?"

He sighed. "The horse will have a new owner."

"I wish your ankle were better." Her eyes filled with worry. It was the sort of gaze that would be better directed at a child on the verge of drowning, and he quickened his strides.

"Don't worry about me. It's as good as new," he lied.

Golden light shone over long strips of clouds, turning the normally gray shade a vibrant lilac. Dabs of snow still sat on the fields, colored reflections amidst murky mud and frosted weeds.

He headed from the barn. He'd been right. His ankle was better: just not, unfortunately, completely improved.

And then he saw it.

The Red Hart.

The very same inn he'd visited on his way to the castle.

The inn would have significantly surpassed the hayloft in comfort and would have lacked sudden morning stress.

"This way." Miles headed toward it, even though the last time he'd visited, he'd been fleeing three women.

"Splendid," Veronique said.

Perhaps yesterday he might have thought it important to remind her that the inn's accommodations would have exceeded that of the barn and that she should have allowed him to search for it, but now the only thing he desired was to bring her relief.

"I'll buy us breakfast and book us on the next mail coach." He hesitated. "This is your last chance to return to your family."

She shrugged. "They'll be happy when they realize I was correct about my baron. Next time I see them, we'll be married."

Her expression shifted to one of wonder, and jealousy prickled through him.

Not that he was actually jealous.

Not that he cared that an engaged woman might desire to spend time with her fiancé.

Not that—

It would be fine.

London might not lie in his preferred direction, and his publisher would be upset when he returned without discovering the identity of Loretta Van Lochen, but he'd never minded the city.

He sighed. All those times he'd been in battlefields, refusing to flee even when some soldiers wielding weapons sprinted at the sight of Bonaparte's troops, but now an assignment about a bloody penny dreadful author would thwart him.

Still. There was no way he could allow her to step onto the mail coach alone.

He would just deliver her to this Austrian baron and then feel satisfaction he'd helped her find happiness and avoided a marriage with her himself.

Once he was in London, he could enjoy the start of the season. His brothers had been mad to suggest he settle down.

Love was ridiculous. Hadn't Veronique's devotion to her fiancé caused her nothing but trouble?

When he opened the creaking wooden door of *The Red Hart*, he half expected to see Miss Haskett and her two charges jump out at him, sketchbooks in hand.

Instead, a few grizzly Scottish locals relaxed in the inn. Evidently they'd aspired to consume as much of the ale and whiskey in the location as they could and were prepared to start early to accomplish the task.

Miles approached the barmaid.

She recognized him at once, and her eyes flared as she saw Veronique, and she grinned. "Will you be wanting the private room this time?"

"That will not be necessary," Miles said.

"I hope you'll eat your meal this time," the barmaid grumbled. "No good insulting Cook."

"Naturally."

She told him the price of the meal, and he reached to remove his purse.

Or at least, he intended to remove his purse.

Somehow it seemed to be missing.

He frowned.

And then his heartbeat quickened. He was in Scotland, without any money, with a woman to care for and—

MAD ABOUT THE BARON 113

The barmaid's face had a decidedly sullen expression on it.

Where on earth was his blasted purse?

He searched his person again. "I had it when I left..."

The barmaid lowered her eyebrows with the same solemnity of a general ordering his men to direct cannons at the enemy. "I already told the kitchen to prepare your food."

"Let me get that." Veronique dropped some coin on the counter. "Perhaps it is with your horse."

The barmaid sniffed. "What man loses his purse and his horse? It's a wonder these English toffs ever successfully invaded us."

Miles narrowed his eyes automatically. Insults were not occurrences he favored, but Veronique only offered him a smile. "Where should we sit?"

"Not upstairs," Miles muttered, remembering his dreadful experience.

The barmaid sniffed. "Naturally not. You require a lot of coin to hire a room here." She glanced at Veronique. "Though pardon me, ma'am, but you do seem to have more than the requisite money."

Veronique smiled. "A requirement when traveling with this man."

The barmaid's shoulders relaxed, and she smiled. "I can see that."

Chapter Thirteen

Miles guided Veronique to a small wooden table in the corner. Long dark timbers stretched across the ceiling, seeming to split and buckle under the weight of the second story.

Veronique tilted her head upward, and her eyes sparkled. "How old."

"Most people do not display the same degree of wonder at dilapidated dwellings." Miles smiled.

"Pity." Veronique placed her reticule on the table. "How much of life they must miss."

Miles picked up the faded velvet bag and glanced inside. "The barmaid was correct. You do have a remarkable abundance of coin there. I will of course repay you when we arrive."

Veronique shrugged. "Oh, you needn't. I'm dragging you to London after all."

"The trip will not be without expenses."

"Please do not worry."

"I suppose coin is of no concern to you," he said.

Veronique gave him that little mysterious smile of hers again. "Exactly."

He leaned back and nodded. Being correct was not a novel state for him. Still, something in the amusement of her gaze made uncertainty trickle through him, as if he was the only one who didn't know a joke.

Was it possible she thought that was not a lot of money?

Veronique's father was wealthy, of the filthy American variety. Men who made their way to the West Indies tended to have one goal: the procurement of riches.

Still, most fathers didn't give their daughters, no matter how wealthy they were, much pin money.

Money was something for stewards to handle. It was not something to give young women, even of the foreign variety.

Most men possessed little confidence in women's ability to do math, and they certainly had no confidence in a woman's desire to do so.

Women didn't require coin when they visited the haberdasher or tailor. Anyone with any sense, a trait Englishmen tended to possess, would allow them to purchase under their father's names, confident their fathers would pay at the end of the quarter.

Had Veronique stolen the money? Helped herself to her father's purse?

He frowned. Somehow he struggled to imagine her doing so. But she had escaped from the castle...

Veronique tilted her head at him, but he looked away. Something about the curve of her profile, something about her expression and the sense of confidence she had, made him wonder.

He was used to women who gave him flirtatious glances. Women, he supposed, came in two types: there were the confident ones, and then there was the shy variety, composed of new debutantes who giggled and whose skin pinkened whenever he entered the room, as if they were on a sunny beach coast, and he was the bloody sun.

It was the sort of thing that could make a man uncomfortable, and though he appreciated it, he never really took them seriously. After all, there was one thing he was certain of, and that was that there was no bloody way he was the blasted sun.

Veronique was neither of these types. She wasn't overtly flirtatious, and yet she wasn't intimidated by him.

The barmaid came with the food, and he concentrated on eating. Even stale bread could be damned appealing under the right circumstances.

"Were you able to get us space on the mail coach?" Veronique asked finally.

"I did. With reluctance."

She laughed. "I've heard you complain about Scotland."

"Well. Anyone with any sense would see that England is a far greater place to be, despite my brother's incessant laudation of thick woodland."

She smiled. "Then that's why Lord Braunschweig waited to meet me. He was being more romantic."

"Perhaps," Miles said.

He didn't want to argue with her. He wanted her to remain happy. "Tell me more about your childhood on Barbados."

Veronique's face clouded.

Instantly Miles regretted he'd made this the subject of

his conversation. Anyone with any sense, which clearly did not include him, could see the topic made her uncomfortable.

She frowned. "I wonder what people will make of me here."

He didn't have to ask her what she was thinking about. He knew.

He knew exactly.

He tilted his head. "You're not the only person with your skin color."

She laughed, but this time nothing about the sound was nice. "I know. I've seen them. At least they're not called slaves here."

"It's illegal. I'm glad."

He was ashamed he'd never given much thought to the people of Barbados, to the people of the West Indies, to the people in the New World. He'd been more focused on drawing attention to the cruelties on the continent and the threat of Bonaparte's relentless search for power. He'd ignored that parts of the British Empire contained unspeakable cruelties, even as Britain boasted of a war to rescue the world from the empirical urges of its neighbor.

Miles was accustomed to having servants, and he knew it was not very easy for servants to change their positions. But they never had to deal with anything similar to what the people in the New World had to deal with.

Slavery wasn't lauded in Britain. It certainly wasn't defended here. Slavery was viewed as another sign of Britain's superiority to the New World.

But then Britain did not have fields devoid of sufficient workers. The issue was very nearly the opposite. There were more than enough willing workers. Once the war ended, the country had seemed swarmed with strong men.

At first these men had been giddy at having defeated Bonaparte so successfully, though after a few weeks, and certainly after a few months, they looked distraught, distressed, disturbed.

No, they had land here, but the weather was not as fertile as in Barbados. The weather was often cold, very often rainy, and sometimes, like in 1816, in which England simply had no summer at all, even the most skilled wouldn't have been able to force anything on this island to grow.

"What do you know about your family?" Miles asked.

She drew her hands from the table.

"You're wondering just how much I'm one of them." There was an accusatory note in her tone, and his cheeks warmed, even though they were not in a habit of spontaneous heating.

"You're wondering," she said, "if my family were slaves in a house or if they were toiling in the fields."

"I wasn't."

But maybe she was right. Maybe that was exactly he had been thinking.

"You're wondering the exact shade of my parents' skin," she continued.

"I've met you father," Miles said.

"But not my mother." Veronique hesitated. "I don't remember her. I wouldn't be able to tell you the exact shade of her skin. I wouldn't be able to compare it to tea with a generous serving of milk, or to tea where the milk was entirely absent."

He stiffened.

"Forgive me," he said. "I'm so sorry you never knew her."

"It's funny," Veronique said. "Some people say I was

lucky she died. If she hadn't died, I would still be living in Barbados. My father would never have taken me away from her. He would never have seen the need. He even needed a lot of convincing to take me away with him. I know I'm not supposed to know that. I was lucky. Most people who come to Barbados don't come back."

She took a sip of tea and then set the cup down. It seemed to clang against the saucer, the sound magnified by Miles's distaste at having made her unhappy.

"I was lucky he didn't succumb to the diseases so many sailors succumb to," Veronique continued. "I was lucky my grandmother, when she learned he'd returned to the region, was determined to get an audience with him. I was lucky she was old at the time. I was lucky, some people, many people would say, that she was in bad health, so visibly that even my father, who didn't want to take me with him, was convinced he needed to do so. I was lucky he was raised with some sense of morals. I was lucky he was a good parent. I was lucky he'd actually loved my mother."

"No, most people I met would say I was lucky my mother died, that I never knew her. Otherwise I might be a slave now." A strange expression flitted over her face. "Well, of course I would have been."

He had the strange sense she'd been about to confess something else entirely.

"The mail coach is here," the barmaid announced.

Miles rose reluctantly, and they headed outside into the brisk Scottish cold.

"I may have divulged too much," Veronique said as they neared the mail coach. "For some reason it's easy to speak with you."

He smirked. "At least you agree I have some good qualities."

Veronique's cheeks darkened, and Miles hoped she was thinking about their first meeting.

I am.

He offered her his arm, and they strode toward the carriage. Some of the horses from the barn were hitched to the mail coach. They stomped their hooves, eager to move.

Fluffy clouds moved with a swift rapidity over the woodland and mountain peaks, as if desiring to see as much of the landscape as possible. Birds squawked, fluttering their wings happily. Likely they were in shock at not being drenched as they flew.

Perhaps something in the straightness and steepness of the slopes was appealing.

"My grandmother remains the kindest person I ever met," she said. "I know it must not have been easy for her to give me away when she knew she was dying. I wasn't there for her final weeks."

"I'm so sorry."

Her smile saddened. "I will always regret not being there, just as I'll always remain grateful for the opportunity she gave me. There are uncouth people in every race, every nationality. I merely wish everyone were not afraid of mine. My people mostly worked in the fields, as they were stronger than their paler counterparts who were only suited to be servants inside the house. I should be proud my ancestors were so capable and earned the West Indies so much money, even though they never saw any of it themselves."

He considered his parents. Perhaps society had sneered at their passion, one that had destroyed their mother's previous marriage, but they had been good parents to him and devoted to each other, despite the condescension others of the *ton* gave him.

He wanted to squeeze her hand. She was right.

They stood before the mail coach. Passengers eager to enjoy the rare sunny view had already filled the top deck, and Miles opened the door to the interior.

Veronique stepped inside, and he followed her over the rickety steps. He slid in gratefully to the seat beside Veronique and closed his eyes.

"Why!" a shrill voice called out. "Isn't that Lord Worthing?"

"It's him!" a girlish voice sounded. "Miss Haskett, you can meet him again."

Damnation.

Miles opened his eyes slowly. Perhaps if he slowed the process sufficiently, he would be in London by the time he finished opening them.

Unfortunately neither science nor time worked so helpfully.

Instead all he saw was Miss Haskett.

She did not look happy.

Miles cleared his throat, glancing at Veronique, knowing how unusual they must think it, that he was boarding the coach with another lady.

They knew he was not married.

Maybe he could just ignore her this whole time. Maybe they wouldn't realize they were traveling together.

"Don't dally," a Scottish voice said. "You're the last two to arrive. You made it just in time."

"You know these people?" Veronique asked.

"I do," Miles said miserably.

"I am pleased to meet you." Veronique turned to Miles.

"I was unaware that you were so well acquainted with everyone."

Miles gave her a tight smile, but one of the Fitzroys giggled.

"Lord Worthing is famous," Miss Theodosia Fitzroy said.

"For his proclivity toward grumpiness?" Veronique asked.

They laughed, and Miles shifted in the seat. One of the girls clapped her hands with such vigor that her bracelets, expensive trinkets from the orient, crashed together on her hand, jangling through the crammed carriage.

"He is a hero," Miss Amaryllis Fitzroy said. "He was so adventurous during the war. We all read about his exploits."

"How wonderful," Veronique said.

"Many people were heroes," Miles said. "And most of them fought."

"But did they look as handsome?" Miss Theodosia said.

"Girls!" Miss Haskett sterned her expression, but the women did not look suitably chastened. They were wealthy and their parents had grown accustomed to having other people look after them. Discipline might be an increasingly abstract concept for them.

The task of being a governess for these girls compelled him to feel some sympathy toward Miss Haskett. He shifted his leg, wincing at the sudden pain.

"Did you injure your ankle?" Miss Haskett asked.

"Yes."

"I suppose that is to be expected with your... Lifestyle."

He cringed. The last time he'd seen them he'd been running away.

Miles fought to retain his scowling expression, but for some horrible reason, it seemed bloody difficult to do so in Veronique's presence.

"Are you on your way to London?" Miles asked, changing the subject.

"For our debut," Miss Theodosia Fitzroy said.

"Splendid," Miles said.

"But first we are stopping in a house party in Yorkshire," Miss Haskett said.

"How much traveling you do," Miles said.

Miss Theodosia Fitzroy shrugged. "Miss Haskett felt it important that we see something of Scotland before we marry."

"You are betrothed?" Miles asked.

Somehow the comment only made the girls giggle.

"We will be soon," Miss Amaryllis Fitzroy said. "How could we not?"

Miles nodded. He suspected the sisters had a rather optimistic view of the marital inclinations of the *ton*'s young men.

"Will this be your first time in the city?" Veronique asked.

The sisters laughed again. "Papa is in parliament. We've been there many times."

"How wonderful." Veronique's face brightened. "Do tell me about the city."

Miles should be pleased. He should be ecstatic. She'd dropped speaking about him in favor of geographical questions on England's largest city, but he knew her questions were only so she might imagine her new life with another man.

Chapter
Fourteen

Perhaps Lord Worthing suffered from claustrophobia. The man's ability to retain a pained expression was impressive, given the women's obvious pleasure in seeing him.

The women's perfectly curled locks managed to retain their stiff, immaculate shape despite the sway of the carriage.

"And what is your name?" Miss Haskett asked her. "Lord Worthing should have presented you to us."

Veronique tensed. Admitting she was an unmarried woman, traveling with a man who was not her relative, seemed too final. Perhaps the servants at the castle were already gossiping, certainly Lord Braunschweig would discover when she arrived at his doorstep that she'd acted with great unconventionality, but that didn't mean she wanted the information to go to a strange woman she'd never met.

Lord Worthing sighed. Perhaps that was why he did not want them to speak together.

"Are names really so important?" he asked.

The woman in a stark dark gray dress frowned. "Reputation is a person's most important thing."

Lord Worthing's gaze hardened. "How curious that you do not seem to honor it then."

The woman's cheeks pinkened, and she withdrew a book.

And then Veronique gasped.

The others looked at her, but she was only conscious of the book cover.

Her name, her pen name, her nom de plume, was emblazed in long, swirling curves.

"Oh," she exclaimed. "You're reading a Loretta Van Lochen book."

"You read her too?"

Lord Worthing coughed.

Veronique hesitated. "I've read some books..."

She was conscious of Lord Worthing's gaze on her, and she shifted her legs.

"Indeed. Well then. The colonies cannot be so dreadful," Miss Theodosia Fitzroy said.

Miss Haskett sniffed. "A single solace does not a great nation make."

Miss Fitzroy leaned toward Veronique. "People say she's in this region."

"Oh." Discomfort tightened Veronique's stomach.

They couldn't...know?

Veronique raked her hand through her hair, but halted, deciding that awkward jerky movements would not make her look less guilty. "Why would you think she's here?"

Lord Worthing had thought the same thing, but being in a carriage filled with people interested in seeing her was not reassuring.

Her voice sounded higher than normal, and her cheeks warmed.

"Oh, there was an article about it in *Matchmaking for Wallflowers*," Miss Fitzroy announced.

Veronique blinked.

"Are you unfamiliar with the illustrious pamphlet?" Condescension filled Miss Haskett's voice.

"Well—" Veronique tried to laugh, even though she felt as if she'd accidentally wandered into a wartime interrogation chamber. "I recently arrived from America..."

"Here's the article about Loretta Van Lochen." Miss Fitzroy passed the pamphlet to Veronique.

Veronique stared at the pages. Women in beautiful clothes, arched to reveal the exact cuts and patterns to interested fabric shoppers and tailors.

She spotted her pen name and read the letter to herself.

Matchmaking for Wallflowers

Lamenting the Anonymity of a Certain Splendid Author

Can there be any writer of greater popularity than Loretta Van Lochen? Governesses throughout England have remarked on finding her books slipped inside French grammar guides. We at Matchmaking for Wallflowers will be spending the colder months clutching hold of her books.

The world-renowned author's last three books were set in Scotland, and we hope that the mysterious author's new fascination with the land's rugged terrain and lax elopement laws might translate to an actual visit by the writer.

Alas, the only information on her which her publisher has shared with us is that she uses a pseudonym.

One day we shall find her, and all women will rejoice.

Until we do, let us just remind you that Matchmaking for Wallflowers *is offering a reward for anyone who produces the true identity of this most famous novelist.*

Veronique's fingers shook when she closed the magazine and returned it to Miss Fitzroy. "How curious."

Her popularity had earned her a substantial amount of money and provided her with a sense of safety she appreciated, but her readers must never discover her identity. Her publisher had made that clear.

"When was the reward announced?" Veronique strove to retain some semblance of calm, and pride rushed through her when she managed to keep her voice from wobbling.

The two Fitzroys frowned, but Miss Haskett didn't hesitate. "Two years ago."

"I see." Perhaps Veronique had spent too long writing books about the Highlands. Ever since she'd learned about the lax elopement laws there, she'd dreamed the baron and she might marry there.

That particular dream wouldn't come true, but she would make certain they would marry. And then she would write books set far, far away. Such as Africa. Or the Orient. Likely there were a dearth of books set in Kathmandu.

She resolved not to mention Loretta Van Lochen again.

"Do tell me about Yorkshire. Is there much to see there?"

"They'll be attending a house party," Miss Haskett said. "Sightseeing is an occupation for the lower classes."

"But there must be some things you would desire to see?"

"It is a sign of the horrors of the former colonies that they might possibly believe there is anything of cultural importance in Yorkshire," Miss Haskett said.

"Well there is York Minster," Miss Theodosia Fitzroy mused. "I suppose some people might find that of interest."

Her sister nodded. "The Duchess of Alfriston even started an archaeological project because of the region's supposed abundance of history. She finds the area quite interesting despite the inability of the population to speak in any understandable English." Her cheeks pinkened. "But I suppose as an American might not find incomprehensible English any barrier."

"Exactly," Miss Haskett said with a strident voice she'd likely used to order her charges to study their Latin, or Veronique supposed, their stitching, which might be more likely for them.

"You are fortunate you have been able to visit Britain for even a few weeks. It far surpasses any other country."

"I applaud your confidence," Veronique said. "Though perhaps it comes naturally to a woman whose only experience of travel is in an uncomfortable carriage."

The governess's eyes narrowed, but she remained silent.

Chapter Fifteen

The coach swept through the Scottish Highlands, climbing steep inclines only to follow the winding lane down the other side. Snow dotted rocky peaks, and their reflections glittered in clear lochs. Swathes of fog fluttered over the water, imbuing the area with the sort of romanticism that had probably driven Loretta Van Lochen straight here.

He peeked out the window, as if to spot some quill clutching authoress he might leap out to interview, but it was hopeless.

Currently Miles remained more known for the supposed symmetry of his facial features than for his articles, their function fading from memory, despite the effort it had taken him to research and write them.

Perhaps clinging to his career was mad. His reputation had been strong once, and that was a greater triumph than most might experience. His lips twitched. The fact workers at gaming hells did not know his face would be considered a victory for some of the *ton*.

He sighed.

It didn't matter. He would ensure he delivered Veronique to her fiancé.

The coach slowed, and the driver announced a stop at the next posting inn. Miss Haskett and her charges swept past them.

"Shall we go inside?" he asked Veronique

Veronique tilted her head. "You're not fond of the others."

"Well—"

"Why not?" Her question was so blunt, that he blinked.

Most of the *ton* didn't ask such direct questions. If they were curious about something they would ask their servants or friends, by which time whatever gossip they wanted to obtain seemed to grow to a larger significance, if only by involving more people in it.

"They are perhaps overly interested in my name," he said finally. "The mere fact that both the Miss Fitzroys and I might be invited to the same events does not indicate we have things in common." Miles flushed. Confessing emotions to practical strangers was not a practice he advocated. Still, even though Veronique and he had only met two days ago, they'd spent far too long discussing things. More perhaps, than he even spoke about with his brothers.

"Let's find a post chaise," Veronique announced.

He frowned. "Excuse me?"

"Someone must desire to drive us. A mail coach cannot be our only option."

"But any other option would be most expensive," he said carefully.

She gave him another mysterious smile. "So be it."

He followed after her. "You need not hire another form of transport for my sake."

She shrugged. "If it will take us over a week to get to London, I would rather do so under the most pleasant possible circumstances."

"Why don't we just purchase a post chaise," he joked.

Her eyes widened. "That's a brilliant idea."

"Really?" Miles rather liked his ideas to be bestowed with labels asserting their brilliance, but he hadn't considered that spending vast amount of coin would render such enthusiasm.

"You can be the driver."

"We'll need to hire new horses every fifteen miles," Miles said.

She hesitated. "Do your capabilities extend that far?"

He frowned. "Naturally."

Her eyes glimmered, and he had the curious sense that she'd only feigned doubt in his abilities to equal that of coach drivers.

Veronique marched toward the groom, and her plain dark dress, likely chosen for its suitability for horse riding, swept against him. He turned his head. No use contemplating her elegant strides over the gravel.

He smirked. Perhaps the other ladies of the *ton* were so shielded that a fallen twig in their path would be a sign for concern. Perhaps her childhood, wandering about on a tropical island as her grandmother toiled had made her more self-reliant. A puddle was not an occasion to reach for a gentleman's arm, when she might evade it quickly herself.

Miles contemplated Veronique as she approached the men. Even in this it seemed to have never occurred to her to let him handle these administrative matters. An independent spirit was not a quality he was accustomed to encountering in high society women, unless it was to spend more than their allotted allowance despite their husbands' wishes.

The groom's eyebrows darted up.

Miles smiled. Veronique must have declared her intention of buying transport.

The groom fetched another man, and after some animated discussion, judging from the frequent movement of their hands, Veronique waved at him. "All settled."

"How quick." Miles joined her, and he smiled.

"The sooner to get to London," Veronique said, her dark eyes sparkling.

Miles averted his gaze, lest he linger too long on the shards of gold that danced in her eyes.

"This way." A Scotsman led them to a canary colored post chaise. "Ain't ever seen such people in a hurry. This will save you the trouble of changing in Glasgow."

Miles and Veronique murmured their thanks, and the groom hitched up two horses.

Miles climbed onto the left horse, and Veronique entered the post chaise. She spread her skirts over the two seats, and he couldn't help but glimpse her triumphant smile.

Perhaps her generosity hadn't been entirely without benefit to her.

Miles wasn't certain how he'd given up his assignment to take on the role of driver, but he was certain he didn't like it.

Much.

The scent of fresh air, mingling with that of pine trees, contrasted favorably to the liberal dousing of perfume, supposedly formed with the most unctuous portions of whales in order to best preserve the equally questionable floral scent.

Unlike their Mayfair counterparts, the horses did not appear as if they'd been bred for delicate limbs, and they jaunted easily up the hill, likely relieved to not be toiling in a rocky field, and to be cantering on some semblance of a path.

The Highlands spread before him, and the gray sky was replaced with pink and orange beams. The steep hills seemed to darken in contrast, as if to allow the viewer to marvel at their shape.

It had been actually damned good of Veronique to do this. Thank goodness she was not one of the prim and proper ladies of the *ton* who went about quoting etiquette rules with the vigor of an actor reciting Shakespeare.

He'd make sure she was well and sorted in London. Take her to the church himself.

Miles pulled into a tiny public house. Only a few carriages were scattered before the inn, and the light from the windows emitted a dim orange glow. "This should suffice."

"Last time you said that I was sleeping on hay," Veronique said, but he couldn't miss the amusement in her tone.

Veronique slipped him some coin, and Miles spoke with the innkeeper. The few locals, perhaps unimpressed with the meal and ale offerings, seemed hardly the type to go storming rooms in search of a lone woman, and he arranged for two rooms.

Veronique followed him up a narrow staircase, and he opened the door to her room.

"I've asked the landlady to send up some food for you from the kitchen," he said.

"Thank you." She smoothed a section of her hair. The action was nonsense. Her hair always looked divine, and she averted her gaze from him. "Where will you dine?"

"Downstairs," he said. "I want to ask the locals if they've heard any rumors about Loretta Van Lochen."

"Oh." Her expression remained inscrutable. Clearly she remained unimpressed with his work. He sighed. She'd been inside the post chaise, and they hadn't had much time to speak more.

"I would invite you," Miles said, "but it's not every day people here see a beautiful girl."

She nodded slowly. "I see."

"Wish me luck," he said.

"Naturally," Veronique said after a pause, and he headed toward the sound of the pub.

*

Veronique lowered her eyelashes, conscious her heart was beating with an unnecessary vigor.

Men didn't give her compliments.

The men in Salem knew the rumors of her background, and on the few occasions when she'd been in public, she'd caught their gazes on her, as if assessing the width of her nose and shade of her skin to compare them to their families' slaves.

But Lord Worthing knew about the rumors, knew the veracity of the rumors, and yet he still called her beautiful.

She smiled.

He hadn't once spoken demeaningly of people "like her."

He hadn't even given her the vague compliments that some people did when attempting to be nice. He hadn't praised her people's singing or their superiority at hauling huge packets upon their backs.

Veronique locked the door and settled onto the bed, willing her heart beat to normalize.

Guilt that she hadn't told Lord Worthing her identity swept over her. She despised that he was spending the evening searching for Loretta Van Lochen, not knowing that she was right here.

She sighed. But it would be unfair to tell him the truth and then to tell him not to share the news with his publisher. She couldn't let a man like him know who she was.

If her identity was revealed, if everybody learned they were reading the stories of a mulatto from Barbados—well, perhaps her publisher was correct in supposing that the sales of her stories would dwindle.

And she couldn't let that happen.

Writing her stories was the dearest thing in the world to her. She wouldn't permit anyone to take that opportunity away. Even if the man was kinder than she'd expected.

Lord Braunschweig, she reminded herself sternly.

Any favorable thoughts on men should be relegated to him.

Perhaps he hadn't made it to their wedding—that didn't mean he was bad husband material, did it? That simply meant he struggled with some time management issues. And time management was not everything—was it? If it was, every woman in high society would be eloping with their father's steward.

No, she was marrying Lord Braunschweig because he was good and wonderful.

He might have forgotten the date of their wedding, or perhaps something else had delayed him, but when Veronique saw him, all would be wonderful and they would live happily ever after.

She smiled, lulled into sleep by her peaceful thoughts.

Chapter Sixteen

The days passed quickly, and Veronique and he settled into a routine. During the day she rode in the back, while he guided the horses. The steep inclines of the Highlands succumbed to smaller hills, and wagons, likely bound for London, frequented the road.

No one seemed to know about any authoress, but Miles was certain he knew who the person was.

Thankfully, he'd already met her.

Once he went to London, he could do more research and find proof.

Even if Loretta Van Lochen had recently developed an interest in Scotland, none of her previous books were set there. In fact most of her books were set in the glittering balls of London. What better person to write about it than someone on the fringes of society?

Yes, he knew exactly the person.

Loretta Van Lochen was someone who frequented London, who visited other locations with her charges, and who even was in Scotland on an excursion.

What person kept track of when rewards for people were issued in certain pamphlets?

A person who wanted to evade discovery.

It had been odd that Miss Haskett had had so much information on Loretta Van Lochen.

He was quite sure that Miss Haskett was Loretta Van Lochen. After all, she was prone to being overly romantic. He'd always supposed Miss Haskett to be clever. If only she did something worthwhile with her intellect rather than scolding young girls and speaking derisively of others. He'd heard enough demeaning comments when people spoke of his parents, as if no one cared that they'd both passed on. Writing penny dreadfuls did not qualify as a worthwhile occupation.

Bang.

The coach tilted, and he forced himself to keep the post chaise on the road, steadying the horses as they whinnied. The coach plopped downward.

Blast.

"Lord Worthing?" Veronique cried.

Miles jumped from his seat, ran over the muddy ground and opened the carriage door. His heart raced. "Are you injured?"

"No. Just startled. What happened?"

He sighed. "The horses were startled by a hunter. You mustn't worry. Just need to get the horses back on the road."

Her face remained serious. "The roads have gotten worse."

"Perhaps."

"We should move to a mail coach," she said. "You shouldn't be doing all of that work."

"If you're certain..."

"You've been wonderful," Veronique said, and his heartbeat quickened more than it should have at her words.

After another night at an inn, where they slept in two rooms as they always did, they took the mail coach toward London.

He almost missed the Fitzroy sisters and Miss Haskett. The heavyset male passengers who spoke of the weather in thick Essex accents seemed more intimidating.

Veronique's shoulders tensed, and Miles sighed. Strangers would hold more danger to her than to other people.

The men, though, chatted merrily about their businesses, and the coach jostled forward.

*

The fields grew smaller, interspersed with idyllic thatched cottages and windmills at an ever-increasing frequency. No signs of snow were present, and the carriage moved easily over the lane, well-maintained due to its proximity to the capital.

"Reckon we'll be in London by midday," one of the merchants said.

Veronique stifled a yawn, and Miles smiled. "Go to sleep."

She shook her head.

"My shoulder makes a good makeshift pillow," he whispered.

"That wouldn't be proper..."

He shrugged. "You need to get some rest before you see the baron."

He abhorred using that excuse. He despised thinking

of her pining for a man who hadn't bothered to appear at the chapel to wed her.

But his words were enough for her to nod, enough for her to lean back, and enough for her to tuck herself against his arm. Her long eyelashes fluttered down, and Miles strove not to contemplate the pleasant warmth coming from the feel of her body pressed against his in the crowded carriage.

The buildings thickened, and cobblestones replaced the dirt. The clamors of hackney drivers competing for space on the road and street vendors hawking their wares ousted the occasional bird aria. Horse riders cantered beside the mail coach, and the horses' hooves caused dust to swirl.

Veronique stirred, and Miles smiled at her.

"Welcome to London."

"Oh." Veronique scrambled up and peered out the window.

Brown cloaked men and women padded the streets, their uncombed hair evident as they bargained with street vendors.

"It lacks the sumptuousness of other sections of the city," Miles said carefully.

Veronique sat back. "I adore it. So much energy. Like the marketplaces in Barbados."

Miles smiled. Most women of the *ton* would be fearful of even peering out the window, as if the sight of a velvet portmanteau or feathered hat might compel a passerby to attack a coach in broad daylight before thousands of people.

"Do you know where Lord Braunschweig resides?" Miles asked.

Veronique nodded and opened her bag. "The address is on his letters."

Stacks of neatly tied letters lay in her satchel, amidst her small selection of clothes.

Naturally.

She'd probably memorized the address long ago.

What must it be like to forge such a strong connection with her?

She placed an envelope in his hand. "Do you know where to find this?"

He glanced at the address.

Mayfair.

He nodded. "Yes."

She would soon be living amongst all the *ton.*

Or be broken-hearted to find that the baron did not want to marry her, even if that meant the man was a blasted fool.

Miles needed to speak with her. This was his last chance. Perhaps the baron would usher Veronique into his townhome, and Miles would never see her again.

He told himself this is what he wanted to happen. He wanted her to be happy, and for whatever reason, happiness for Veronique seemed to come from Lord Braunschweig, this Austrian stranger.

Miles considered not saying anything. He shook his head. He'd witnessed too many unhappy marriages over the years. He'd spent too many nights with too many unhappily married women, and he'd attended the clubs where even the supposedly happily married men regaled themselves with stories of this opera singer, or that widow.

The coach stopped, and they stepped onto the cobblestones.

"Let's get a hack." Miles led Veronique to the row of

dusty black carriages. He offered her his hand, and fire sparked through his body.

Not being with Veronique seemed to be a ridiculous idea for his nerve endings, which urged him to sweep her into his arms again.

He sighed.

Should he tell her?

He shook his head. Confusion in her life could not be a welcome addition.

Still...

He couldn't permit her to amble into the man's townhouse with the confidence of a heroine in a fairytale.

For all he knew the man was no diplomat at all, but merely a servant, making good use of his employer's address. A man with the patience to wait for two years to marry a woman he'd never seen before, might lack a pleasurable physique and personality. Heavens, he might be aged, wary of making the journey to Scotland without a good doctor on hand. And even if he were an Austrian baron, who was to say if he'd truly written the letters, or if he'd tasked it to a sister or an overly romantic clerk.

Veronique couldn't wed a man she'd never met before. No one deserved that.

And Veronique—Veronique deserved everything.

Miles cleared his throat. "I would not be doing my duty if I did not warn you—"

"Warn me?" Veronique turned her head, and amusement rippled through her voice. "What foreboding vocabulary you use."

"This is an occasion for that."

Her features stiffened, and he cursed himself. He despised he was spending possibly their last moments together making her uncomfortable.

"Marriage is not an institution to be entered lightly," he said.

"I'm aware of that," she said tersely. "I've been corresponding with Lord Braunschweig for two years."

"Yet he did not make an appearance at your elopement. Perhaps he does not desire to be married to you. Surely you must have considered it. Does he know about—" He did not know how to broach the subject of her heritage, and her eyes darkened with what could only be anger.

She raised her chin defiantly. "I told him. We have no secrets."

"When did you tell him?"

"Well," she paused. "In my last letter, when we discussed the elopement." Her voice faltered. "I know what you must think. And I've pondered it too. But I was so certain...I told him so many other things."

"What other secrets do you have?"

"I wouldn't tell you."

She may as well have slapped him. But why should she tell him her secrets? He stepped toward her and grabbed hold of her wrist.

She stopped in obvious surprise. She was standing still. He should let her go, but his hand just squeezed hers more tightly as if memorizing the exact width of her wrist, and the exact shape of its circumference.

"Perhaps he's simply interested because you're the sister of a duke."

"Stepsister."

"Even if you are not titled, your father is wealthy," he said. "Perhaps he saw you as a financial investment."

"He wouldn't," she said, but her voice wavered. She was listening to him now.

"How do you know this man is truly a baron?"

"I'm sure of it," she said.

"I hope you're right." He felt like he should be saying more to her.

"Love," he said, "is something in stories for little girls."

"What exactly are you trying to say?"

"You might find Lord Braunschweig lacking—"

"In what?" she asked.

"Well..."

"A leg, like the dear Duke of Alfriston?"

"I was thinking a brain for not managing to be at your wedding."

"He may have an excuse." She tossed her hair, and he forced himself not to contemplate the manner in which sunbeams illuminated the strands. "You know absolutely nothing about my relationship with Lord Braunschweig."

"I know men."

"Just because you are devoid of morals does not mean Lord Braunschweig is. I've heard about you, Lord Worthing. Don't think I haven't. I've heard your brothers worry about you before you arrived. That's what they discussed. About how you were a perpetual bachelor, a perpetual rogue."

"Did they say that?" He stiffened.

"Yes."

"I always thought they admired my lifestyle."

"No, it's pathetic. You have everything in the world going for you, but you only complain."

"You know nothing of him," he said. "Perhaps he's aged. Perhaps he's corpulent."

"That won't matter. And you should be more open-minded."

"Me?" He frowned, but perhaps, just perhaps she was

right. Perhaps he was just imagining flaws for Lord Braunschweig. He would find out soon.

She opened her satchel and grabbed a bundle of letters. She thrust yellowed pages into Miles's hands. "Read these. This is from a man who loves me. Who believes in me."

Miles browsed through the paper. Sentimental endearments flashed at him. Endearments that Veronique deserved to hear.

"What do you say now?" Her voice was defiant.

"Just—just prepare yourself."

"So you don't believe—" She glanced at the letters, and her voice was more forlorn.

"I don't know," he said finally. "I do know you deserve to be treated well."

She inhaled. "Is there...anything else you wanted to tell me? Any other reason why I should not go with the baron?"

This was the moment.

This was the time when he might tell her that he'd started to care for her, and the thought of her marrying another man left him curiously pained.

But romance was for other men. He knew how short lived his mother's marriage with her first husband had been.

It would be unfair for him now to do anything to confuse her. Not when she was standing outside her fiancé's home. Perhaps his father had not respected his mother's marriage and pursued her anyway, but Miles would hold himself to higher morals.

"What else could I say?" For some reason his voice wobbled.

Something flickered over her face, and he averted his gaze.

"So this is it," she said finally.

They strolled to the town house. Everything was quiet, a testament to the excellent property. Their feet sounded impossibly loud over the stone gravel, and a servant poked his face in their direction.

This was a beautiful townhouse, he admitted to himself. Even the small garden was pristine. Somehow he'd been expecting that there was no Lord Braunschweig, that there was only a person feigning to be him.

Miles rapped the lion knocker on the glossy ivory painted door.

Perhaps it was some abandoned townhouse, and the gardener was some eccentric gentleman with an unnatural love for plants.

But in the next moment the door swung open, and a man peered at him. "May I help you?"

"We wanted to see Lord Braunschweig," Veronique said. "Or rather—I wanted to see him. I am Veronique Daventry."

She paused, but the butler did not so much as flicker his eyes. "Lord Braunschweig is out."

"Oh." Veronique's shoulders slumped.

Miles sighed. The man was probably cowering upstairs. Clearly he didn't know how to face the woman he'd misled for years. Miles stepped into the corridor, ignoring the sudden flare of the butler's eyes.

"Now, look here, I am Lord Worthing. We have traveled hundreds of miles to see Lord Braunschweig. We intend to see him."

"How very dramatic." The butler rolled his eyes over Lord Worthing, as if assessing his attire.

Miles sighed. Perhaps the days-long carriage ride had made him appear scruffy. He hadn't put on his best when he'd climbed down the castle wall, and he hadn't managed to wash the stains from the pit.

"Lord Braunschweig is not here."

"Oh." Veronique's voice sounded so sad. So pitiful.

"He will not be here for some time, I imagine."

"We are prepared to wait for him." Lord Worthing headed down the corridor. "Please show us to your drawing room at once. Where is it?"

The butler cleared his throat. "Lord Braunschweig is in Scotland, I believe."

"Scotland!" Veronique's eyes widened, and Miles halted.

"Yes," the butler said. "It was a matter of some importance. He'd never been to Scotland before. I don't know why he would be compelled to do so now. The baron said I would be surprised when he returned."

"Oh." Veronique's eyes sparkled, and her normally large vocabulary seemed reduced to a single wondrous moan.

Lord Worthing sighed. He'd been so certain of his poor intentions, but Lord Braunschweig must have been waylaid.

Veronique had been correct to insist the man would arrive, and he'd been bloody awful for attempting to dissuade her.

"Do you by any chance know the path he took?" Lord Worthing asked.

"I suppose I can ask the groom," the butler said.

"That would be wonderful." Miles glanced at Veronique. "Don't worry, we're going to go after Lord Braunschweig."

*

He'd come for her after all.

Veronique's heart thrummed with happiness. Or at least, it should be thrumming with happiness. It would certainly thrum with happiness very soon.

Somehow casting an "I told you so" glance at Lord Worthing did not prove as rewarding as she'd contemplated.

Never mind.

She was just tired at the prospect of a long trip toward Scotland. That was it. It had nothing to do with a thought that perhaps her life's happiness did not rest on Lord Braunschweig's presence in her life after all.

Lord Worthing's face remained grim, and she watched him follow the butler.

She settled down on a stone step underneath the portico. Gilded phaetons and carriages pulled by white horses sauntered down the street, driven by grooms in sumptuous striped uniforms. Trees lined the pavement, their leaves stirring slightly in the breeze, the weather less dramatic than that of Barbados or even Scotland.

Home.

Not yet, but soon.

Once she caught up with Bertrand, they would return here.

Her dreams were coming true.

Somehow the thought did not make her smile.

Lord Worthing returned with the butler. "We'll follow the same path he took. Perhaps we might learn of his whereabouts."

"You don't have to do all of this," she said.

"What do you mean?"

She smiled. "You could find me a chaperone and send

me up alone. You live in London. You must know someone suitable."

"The thought hadn't occurred to me."

Oh. That was nice.

"Would you like me to do that?" Lord Worthing asked carefully.

"I—" She hesitated. Thoughts of being passed around to some efficient chaperone, someone like Miss Hatchett, did not seem enticing.

It was the correct thing to do though.

And Lord Worthing—hadn't she told herself she would be relieved to be rid of him? Hadn't she told him of her discomfort that he'd joined her journey?

And yet...

Not seeing him anymore seemed...odd.

"I suppose you're going in the direction of Scotland anyway..."

He nodded. "Yes, I want to find Loretta Van Lochen."

She attempted not to cringe. "I suppose it might take a while to find someone else... I doubt my reputation can become more damaged."

"Let's go now," he said and strode toward the hack. He waved to the driver, and Veronique had the strange sensation everything would be fine.

Chapter
Seventeen

They moved swiftly toward Scotland. This time they took all their meals together, and Miles did not insist she dine alone in her room.

He'd warned her about Lord Braunschweig, but he'd been mistaken. The man had intended to marry her.

Veronique and he spoke of other things instead, musing over the political situations in the West Indies and the continent. She was intelligent, and it was pleasant to be with a woman so strong-minded, whose knowledge was not confined to selecting haberdashery.

Finally they arrived in Yorkshire, and the coach stopped. The public house squatted on a hill. The stones seemed to buckle underneath the weight of the thatched roof, but light shone from the window, and Miles entered the public house to mail a message to Gerard.

Likely they would arrive at the same time as the letter, but if they were separated from the mail coach, he wanted to assure Gerard that Veronique and he were well and were making their way as quickly as they could.

Perhaps Gerard and the true baron were even conducting search parties through the Highlands for Veronique and him.

Miles pushed away the guilt that swept through him. He was in England, and the thought made him smile. He wouldn't find any overly patriotic Scotsmen traipsing around in tartan, and none of them would speak joyfully at the possibility of scaring Englishmen away with pitchforks and haggis.

He marched to the tired looking publican behind the counter. A swarm of men were inside, and the publican likely had exhausted himself hauling huge tankards of ale to the men.

"Yer a right posh one." An old man gave a toothy grin, oozing the self-satisfaction of a man who'd made it to a sufficiently advanced age that his hair had changed color, and who was bestowed respect from the sheer fact of his continued existence.

Miles shrugged and smiled modestly.

"Reckon 'e's going to the house party on the hill," another man said.

"No parties for me." He put the letter on the table. "I wanted to mail this."

One of the men peered at the address and then his eyes widened. "Yer mailing that to Scotland."

"Yes," Miles affirmed.

"That means he knows people who are Scottish," a burly man said glumly.

"Ah, dear," a white-haired man said. "Reckon you better have a drink then."

"I really shouldn't," Miles said.

"And ponder the misfortune of your acquaintances' heritage without the benefit of ale?" The white-haired man shook his head. "And I thought people were brave during the Napoleonic Wars."

"It's not so tragic," Miles said.

"But you can still drink something." The burly man patted the chair next to him. "Mr. Nicholas and I are used to dealing with people in your class."

"My class?"

"Fancy folks with accents." The burly man shrugged. "We work for a duchess."

"Oh." Miles tilted his head. There was only one duchess in this area. "It wouldn't be the Duchess of Alfriston?"

He knew the Duchess of Alfriston. His brother Marcus was married to her younger sister.

The man beamed. "She is indeed." He shook his head. "It's funny how all these fancy folks know each other, ain't it."

Miles smiled as the men continued to ponder the smallness of their world.

"She's a right nice woman," Mr. Nicholas mused. "We do archaeological work for her." He jutted his thumb at the burly man beside him. "This man is good at digging."

Miles smiled. "I see."

"Yeah, everyone's good at spotting my muscles," the burly man said proudly.

"I didn't know this would be such a hub of activity." Miles glanced around the pub.

"Oh, yes. Why, we had a baron in 'ere recently."

Miles stiffened. "Who?"

"Lord B something or other. Brown, perhaps? Bernard?"

Miles swallowed hard. "It wouldn't be Lord Braunschweig?" He ordered a tankard of ale.

The man slapped his knee. "Yer right! I told you, you posh people all be knowing one another."

"I've never actually met the person." Miles was suddenly grateful when his drink arrived, and he took a long swig of ale, though the prickly sensation of bubbles against his throat didn't quite manage to soothe him. "What was he like?"

"Oh, solemn fellow," Nicholas mused. "Right proper. He weren't drinking ale like you."

"I see." Miles took another sip of his ale. It didn't surprise him that Lord Braunschweig was the proper type.

Had he had second thoughts on Veronique?

"When did you see him?"

"Ah, reckon it was last Tuesday. Three nights past."

Lord Worthing nodded. The man could be anywhere. Up in Scotland or well on his way to Cornwall.

"But you can see 'im yerself if you like," Mr. Nicholas said. "'E's at Lady Mulbourne's."

"Lady Mulborne?"

"Just down the road from 'ere. She's 'aving a house party. There's a ball tonight."

"Indeed?"

Mr. Nicholas looked surprised. "I'm sorry, sir. I assumed that's where you was going. Ain't *that* often we see fancy folk like you 'ere."

Miles finished his drink. "That's a pity. It's quite pleasant here." He smiled. The men were very nice. "I might stop by the house party though."

He arranged for accommodation and then went to fetch Veronique.

*

Veronique stuffed some papers in her packet as he approached. Likely she was composing love letters to the baron.

He sighed.

"Did you manage to mail the letter?" she asked.

He nodded, his glance solemn, and her smile wobbled. Miles sighed.

He had to tell Veronique.

"I found him," he said.

She blinked, but she didn't ask who.

His heart toppled downward, and he wondered despite himself just how much Veronique thought about Lord Braunschweig. The baron had been charming her for two years.

"Where is he?" Veronique asked.

"Not far from here. He's at an—" Miles looked down. He couldn't look her in her eyes. "He's at a house party."

Veronique's eyes widened momentarily, and then she flung her gaze downward. "I see."

"Perhaps he was on the way to see you and got...waylaid." The excuse sounded weak to him, but Veronique nodded, more happily now.

Miles abhorred that the man was so close.

If Miles had made the journey to see his brother, Lord Braunschweig certainly should have been able to travel past Yorkshire.

"You can see him tonight," Miles said.

"Splendid," Veronique said.

Miles thought she might have said that a trifle weakly, but he decided the usual force of her words may have been hampered by the wind, and his own distracted mind.

"We'll go this evening. I learned they're having a ball there."

Veronique's face fell. "I'm not dressed for a ball. My attire is most suited for travel."

"On horseback? By yourself?" Miles smiled, and he tucked a stray lock that had fallen from Veronique's hair behind her ear.

He stepped away.

He shouldn't be so familiar with her.

He shouldn't remember the feel of her lips against his with such clarity, and he shouldn't desire to pull her toward him.

His embrace wouldn't comfort her. The only person she craved was Lord Braunschweig.

And Miles had the horrible feeling Lord Braunschweig was wholly unworthy of her.

He cleared his throat. "Let's go."

"I've never even been to a ball," she said. "I hoped our first meeting would be...nicer."

He nodded. She'd looked exquisite in her dress when he first met her.

"You've never been to a ball?"

She shook her head.

"But they do have those in Boston."

"My family lived in Salem. But yes, they do have those in Boston."

He still looked at her strangely, and she sighed.

"My stepmother didn't want me to attend one. She thought my presence might distract from that of her daughters. They were wallflowers."

He nodded. "I see."

"I mean, it was right for her to be concerned. You can see why people might talk about me, and well, the colonies are not as comfortable with people of my kind as people are in England. Or at least, I hope they are in England."

"You should have been there. Your father is an important man. He shouldn't have distinguished between you and your sisters. That doesn't help people learn anything, if they fear people of your complexion"

"They wouldn't call it fear," she said.

"I think they're scared. Of the strength, the power, that they associate with the slaves in the south and the Caribbean. Nothing is going to change if you don't put yourself out there to help people to change."

She tilted her head.

, she's so pretty.

"You mean how you went to the continent to report on the war even though very few people were doing that, and all the enemies must have supposed you a spy?"

"Something like that. Though I would not wish discomfort on you. But a ball, with your family?" He shrugged. "I don't know. If you had been prepared for the occasional gossipy comment and mean-spirited language? I think you should have gone. I'm sorry, I don't need to agree with your father on everything."

She laughed, still staring at him.

"I'll find a dress for you."

She looked at him strangely. "And just how are you supposed to do that? It takes ages for a seamstress to make something, and..." she smirked, "...you've forgotten your purse."

"Nothing will stop me. Besides, I know people."

"Is that so?" she asked.

He nodded. "I'll arrange something for you."

*

Ballgown selection might be a task relegated to others with more experience bargaining with haberdashers, perusing fashion prints, and maintaining some knowledge of color theory and trends, but if Veronique desired a gown, Miles would find one for her. No matter that gowns took weeks, even months, to make.

The leaves, pale green imitations of summer's emerald finery, did not fully adorn the trees yet, and Lady Mulborne's estate was easily visible. Men in tweed jackets escorted women toting ruffled parasols through the gardens. Some entered the medieval maze and others seemed content to marvel at the rose bushes, not yet in bloom, perhaps seizing the chance to display a mastery of botany and fearlessness at the prospect of pronouncing lengthy Latin words.

A few men nodded to him and the rise of the women's smiles were visible even underneath their bonnets' generous brims.

Miles didn't linger.

He marched up the steps and pounded on the door. The butler open promptly, evidently accustomed to the incessant exit and entrance of guests.

"Lord Worthing." The butler tilted his torso in a dignified bow. "I was not aware you would grace us with your presence."

"I need to see Lady Mulborne."

"Ah."

"At once."

The butler's composed countenance didn't wobble. "Please let me show you to the parlor."

"I know the way," Miles said. "You can get her."

"Of course," the butler murmured, and Miles didn't

move his head to see if the man still managed to retain his serenity.

This was an emergency.

He stormed into the parlor, startling an overly amorous couple and the woman's sleeping aunt. He paced the room as the pink-faced couple declared their immediate intention to amble the garden.

Finally the door creaked open.

"Lady Mulborne," the butler announced loftily, and Miles swung around.

"How pleasant you should be here," Lady Mulborne said smoothly, but Miles flickered an impatient hand.

"Yes, yes. I hope I can go to your ball tonight. And—er—bring someone."

Lady Mulborne arched a delicate brow. "I am honored you are so eager to attend."

"And I need a dress," Miles continued. "The prettiest you can find."

"Excuse me?"

"It's for my—er—companion. She didn't bring one. And I told her I could get one."

"Well. That is an unusual request."

"And an urgent one," Miles said.

Lady Mulborne hesitated. "Very well. What does she look like?"

"Oh." Miles sighed, and a wave of emotion that he couldn't immediately place swept through him. "Like an angel."

Lady Mulborne's eyes sparkled. "You must give me more information than that. Is she my size? Will she fit in my dresses?"

"She's slender," Miles mused, "though not without curves."

He demonstrated the alluring sweep of her form, but for some reason the action only seemed to cause the woman's smile to widen and he dropped his hand down. "Her skin is a tawny beige but in the right light it glistens with jewel undertones. And her hair—   , her hair is so curly."

"Indeed."

"It's important that the gown be beautiful. She deserves to have a beautiful gown."

For some reason Lady Mulborne covered her lips with her palm. "I take it she is most important."

"Yes."

"I'll find something suitable for her," Lady Mulborne said. "Heaven knows I have plenty of gowns."

"Thank you."

"Will you announce a betrothal by any chance?" Amusement seemed to ripple through her voice. "I have rings too if you need one. I found the most delightful sapphire and diamond ring on my last visit to Venice."

"Well." Miles's shoulders sank somewhat. "Perhaps there will be a formal announcement. She is betrothed."

"To you?"

He shook his head.

"Not yet?" Lady Mulborne's eyes definitely seemed to be sparkling more than normal. Perhaps it was the light.

"To...another man."

Lady Mulborne blinked. "I'm so sorry." She frowned. "It is worthwhile to fight for happiness."

Miles forced away a sudden jolt of pain and laughed. "She's already happy."

And tonight she'll meet her fiancé.

Chapter
Eighteen

A majestic minuet sounded from an open window as Veronique took Lord Worthing's hand and exited the carriage.

Tall hedges, exquisitely shaped in perfectly straight lines, towered on either side of them, but it was the stately home before her that grasped her attention.

Stone gods and goddesses were carved into the facade, and others perched over the water, shooting rivulets into the marble pools.

"It's like a fairytale," Veronique breathed.

Lord Worthing shrugged. "Rather too English for that. Perhaps like one of those places depicted in Miss Van Lochen's books."

She blinked, but when she turned to him, he smiled. He'd seemed quieter ever since he'd fetched the dress. Perhaps he worried she might fail to blend in.

Veronique strode in the gown Lord Worthing had procured for her. The gems sparkled under the moonlight as if she'd been confused with a princess. She looked to see if a window was open, but perhaps the musicians were playing with such force that the quartets spilled easily into the garden.

Smaller buds dotted the bushes and manicured lawn.

The sky was an endless gray, but the steel color seemed to only highlight the garden further. Gravel glistened under the light, leading to statues swathed in exquisite gowns for eternity. The statues stood before a tall hedge, joined by a wrought iron gate.

Veronique inhaled the floral scent. "Is that a maze?"

"It is," Lord Worthing said.

"How heavenly."

She'd dreamed about an event like this. She'd written about it often. Many of her heroines were frequent participants in balls, but she had never attended one herself.

"I'm not ready for this," she said, and her heartbeat pattered an anxious melody.

"You're beautiful," Lord Worthing said. "Lord Braunschweig is a fortunate man."

"Thank you," she murmured, but it came out more like a croak.

For a moment she'd almost imagined she were merely attending the ball with Lord Worthing, as if that were simply something they did on nights when the moon was full and hostesses scheduled events, confident their guests could find them.

A groomsman appeared for their carriage. Veronique tried to look authoritative, as if it were a common occurrence for her to be standing outside a manor house like this.

She'd never been in one of Barbados's few stately

homes, constructed with tiny windows that obscured the view, so the occupants might still imagine they were in Britain. There were some pleasant homes in Massachusetts, though they tended to be constructed with wood, as if the occupants did not care if the next hurricane hauled the planks and planted them in the sea.

This home looked like it would be here for all eternity.

Her feet crunched over the gravel, and she squeezed the silk bag Lord Worthing had given her that contained satin slippers.

"Take my arm," Lord Worthing said. "You'll be fine."

He led her inside, and women's faces seemed to brighten when they saw him. Several people greeted him, slapping his back and murmuring names of people she'd never heard of.

She looked around, wondering which person was Lord Braunschweig.

Her heart tightened. She should be feeling joy, but instead she simply felt uneasy.

"I'll find him for you," Lord Worthing said, and she nodded.

She grasped her fan with fuller force than the delicate handle required and shifted her feet over the gleaming floor. Footmen in ivory wigs marched authoritatively through the room, and men and women stood in clusters, their laughter echoing easily through the ballroom.

Soon Lord Worthing arrived with another man. "May I introduce Lord Braunschweig, Baron of Wolbert."

It was strange that despite how often Lord Worthing had misspoke the baron's name, he uttered it correctly this time, as if he'd listened to her all along.

"Ah, Miss Daventry." She was vaguely aware of golden hair and a tall figure. "Or should I say, Miss Van Lochen?"

She tensed, and her gaze flicked to Lord Worthing. The man had acted more stiffly ever since entering the ball, but now his eyebrows soared upward, and his eyes widened. He seemed to steady himself, but his confusion seemed to have been replaced by anger.

He'd heard Lord Braunschweig's appellation.

He knew her secret.

He knew she'd refused to tell him.

Her heart tumbled downward. He shouldn't have to learn from a stranger. Not when...

She hesitated. After this ball, she wouldn't need to travel with Lord Worthing anymore. Lord Worthing and Lord Braunschweig were not friends. When would she ever see him again?

"You're the authoress," Lord Worthing said.

"Zis is a clever woman," Lord Braunschweig said gladly.

"That is a secret," she said sternly, and she tried to give an apologetic look to Lord Worthing.

She should have told him. She really should have.

"Ach, of course. I thought zis man knew. Is he your brother?"

She frowned. Her stepsister Louisa was married to the man's half-brother's sister. "A relative."

Lord Worthing inhaled sharply. His face seemed to have turned to stone. His chiseled features were unmoving, as effective as any mask. "I should go."

The man disappeared swiftly into the crowd.

She told herself it didn't matter and directed her attention to Lord Braunschweig. She'd been so concerned with Lord Worthing that she'd barely noticed him at all.

"You're truly Lord Braunschweig?" Perhaps she'd

called him Bertrand in her thoughts, but it seemed improper to refer to him by his first name now.

"Ach, yes."

"Splendid." Veronique didn't want her voice to wobble. This was the happiest moment of her life.

But somehow, her voice still wobbled, and she found herself glancing at Lord Worthing, even though all her energy should be focused on Lord Braunschweig, her actual fiancé, and not some man who'd kissed her in some rakish throes of passion.

She peered at her husband-to-be. His profile was exquisite. His features were perfectly symmetrical. His hair was blond and tousled, as if he'd just ventured from a wind-swept manor home, though since the night was not windy, and he'd unlikely taken to rambling the countryside on the way to the ball, it was likely the result of an expert valet.

"It is a pleasure to finally meet my fiancée," Lord Braunschweig said before dipping into a lengthy bow.

Veronique's heart fluttered. If there had been any doubt that Lord Braunschweig wanted to marry her, it had disappeared. "It's a pleasure to meet you too."

"Mm-hmm..." He murmured something and then grasped her hand and kissed it.

His lips were cold, but likely that just contrasted with the warmth soaring through her heart—the warmth she would be feeling soon.

"You are prettier than I expected," Lord Braunschweig said, clipping each syllable and speaking with the concentration of a man still not fluent in a language.

"Why, thank you." His comment made her uneasy, but she smiled. Not everyone was skilled with words.

She'd met him. She'd finally met him. This was her

husband-to-be. This was her true love. They would soon be spending the rest of their lives together in blissful, utter happiness.

"Er—" Lord Braunschweig shifted his legs and raked a hand through his glorious hair. "The vezar is nice."

She blinked, but then supposed he meant "weather" and nodded. "Yes. I'm glad it stopped raining."

"Was it raining?" Lord Braunschweig looked crestfallen. "I—er—must have forgotten."

"Oh."

"But they do tell me that rain is good for farmers." He pushed out his chest and beamed, as if he'd valiantly defended his country. "So you see, my statement was correct."

"Indeed?"

"Yes. The vezar was fine." He paused, as if flummoxed how to proceed now they'd tackled the climate.

She braced herself any moment for a discussion on the quality of the drapes or the sturdiness of the marble floor.

"Shall we dance?" he asked.

"Very well."

He offered her his arm, and they strolled through the room. She had questions. She had so much she wanted to ask him.

"Why weren't you in Scotland? I-I was waiting for you." Her cheeks pinkened at the memory.

He flickered his hand in the air. "Too far. I imagined you weren't serious. I sent a note to you to meet me here. Did you receive it?"

"No. I went to find you. I was...very worried."

He shrugged. "No worries now."

Perhaps the note had at least eased her family's confusion when she'd disappeared. She wouldn't put it past her stepmother to stop anyone from searching from her once she found out that Lord Worthing was likely traveling with her.

"The dance is starting," he said. "We can't be late."

Clearly Lord Braunschweig was aware that they would have the rest of their lives to learn everything about each other, and there was no reason to hurry the process.

They were soon gliding about the dance floor. Veronique bit her lips together. She did like dancing. She'd enjoyed the dance lessons with her stepsisters more than Louisa and Irene had. But that said, she did not have a lot of experience dancing *outside* the confines of her father's and stepmother's ballroom. Other dancers had been a theoretical concept for her. She concentrated on the moves, glancing frequently at the other dancers to mimic what they were doing, and tried to keep count during this English song, one she'd never heard before.

Her heart hammered, probably because she'd just met the love of her life. Not because he'd put her in an uncomfortable situation.

This was the start of the rest of her life. This was romance, dancing in a beautiful dress with all these people. They probably were not thinking about her imperfect dance skills.

She glanced around the ballroom. The crystal sconces sparkled under the candlelight. Gold-framed paintings gleamed under the light, the jeweled attire of the figures still striking, despite the vast competition within the ballroom.

Perhaps London gatherings were crowded, but this was Yorkshire, and there was ample room to observe.

Some wallflowers sat near the fireplace in one corner, flickering longing looks in the directions of a group of men jesting over brandy. The hostess, attired in a striking aubergine gown, perhaps to denote some semblance of half-mourning, fluttered between the guests and the white wig and glossy uniform adorned servants.

Veronique had the vague sense the moment had been carefully orchestrated. The choice of fast-tempoed music, the hours of practice by the bow wielding musicians, the selection of food and drink to best imbue the guests with a happy mood, the careful training of footmen to remain invisible even as they helped the other guests, the gathering of flowers and greeneries to further brighten the already vibrant space: everything had conspired to make the evening perfect.

Had any of her heroines been gifted with as pleasant an occasion for their first dances with their heroes?

"Zis way," Lord Braunschweig said in an almost exasperated tone. "It's a new dance."

Veronique shook her head, as if the action might usher her from her reverie. She shouldn't be contemplating her fiction now. She should be rejoicing that she was finally in the man's company.

She'd battled such odds, crossing foamy oceans, clattering down castle walls, riding a new horse over a new terrain, to experience this moment now.

Other people lined up, and Veronique took her position beside the other women. A few shot her disapproving glances, and she stiffened. Could they tell her heritage? Might they find her unworthy of standing beside them?

Perhaps they merely recognized her as a stranger.

She forced her gaze to contemplate Lord Braunschweig's features, fighting an absurd, unwanted desire to seek out Lord Worthing for assurance. They were merely friends, and soon, when she was married to Lord Braunschweig, ensconced in some Yorkshire home, they would no longer be even that.

She still swung her gaze about the ballroom, past the towering men in silken cravats and jeweled waistcoats, and past the less looming, but equally imposing women, arrayed in shimmering jewels, to seek him out.

Lord Worthing's face was restrained, and he lingered by the appetizer table, even though there were all manner of sweetly attired women with whom he might dance. Where was the man's easy smile now?

The music sounded and too late she noticed the dancers were already moving. She hastened to join them as they leaped to the joyful tune of a flute, resisting the urge to return to Lord Worthing's side.

"Not used to dancing?" Lord Braunschweig asked.

"I—"

She firmed her jaw. She was a good dancer. She just needed to...concentrate on the music.

The man grinned. "Do as I do."

Her legs felt unsteady, and she had a great sympathy for newborn fawns urged by their mothers to amble about. Her heart seemed to be more preoccupied in palpitating against her ribs than in issuing steady breaths.

Still, she followed the women as they formed new patterns. This was what she'd dreamed of, but she felt fraudulent on the dance floor. Her gloved hands might touch theirs at the requisite moments, but she wasn't one of them.

None of them had grown up under the hot tropical sun that beat down relentlessly over Barbados. None of them had played with dark-skinned children and gone home to a grandmother who would never be accepted into even the lowest rungs of white society.

Likely they'd all attended the same dance lessons, played in the same impeccable gardens, and gotten lost in the same immaculately trimmed labyrinths in the safety of their father's massive and well-guarded estates.

The music halted, and she cast a wobbly smile at Lord Braunschweig. The man's face had grown still rosier, and he wiped a hand over his now greasy coiffure.

"Time for some punch!" he exclaimed.

"Splendid," she said weakly.

He frowned. "Lemonade for you, my dear. I'm not a proponent of alcohol for women. Some things should be left to men. Our bodies are naturally equipped to imbibe brandy and wine."

"Oh." She felt as if she were being scolded by a schoolmaster. The drink was never anything she'd given any particular thought to, but now that it was forbidden, she missed it. "I think women are equally capable."

"Even though good brandy might burn their delicate throats?" He uttered a short laugh.

She blinked, and Lord Braunschweig continued to the punch table. Vibrant drinks sparkled in crystal jugs and guests dipped silver ladles through the spice-scented liquid.

The other guests seemed to turn away from Lord Braunschweig when he approached, and Veronique's heart slid further downward, tangling with her stomach, and filling her with an uneasy dread.

She'd spoken with Lord Braunschweig. It wasn't unfathomable that others of the *ton* might feel reluctant to converse with him. Perhaps that was the reason he'd been so willing to send her all those letters. The fact he had not married for two years might not be necessarily attributed to a deep, romantic faithfulness after all. The process of finding a wife must be a greater challenge to those who struggled to find a conversation partner.

She frowned. Where was Lord Worthing?

The other men lounged comfortably against the punch table, secured perhaps by both alcohol and the frequency with which they'd danced in this ballroom on past occasions. Some women, perhaps their wives, perhaps simply aggressive debutantes emboldened by their lady's maids and doting mamas' effusive compliments on their appearances, stood nearby.

Veronique tossed her hair, conscious her locks would fall in a pleasing manner. Unlike her stepsisters, she'd never lacked confidence in her appearance. Though she could not remember her mother, she'd seen a painting of her. There was a reason her father had fallen for her mother, despite her unconventional background, and she had little doubt that reason lay in symmetrical features and a slender figure.

They don't know, she reminded herself.

Gossip in Massachusetts would not be familiar to these women. They likely didn't even know her name, and though some people suspected that her complexion might be somewhat too dark, it never occurred to most people that anyone attired in a dress such as hers could have a risqué background.

She held her head high and grabbed a glass of punch that some helpful footman had already poured. Tiny fruits floated in the rum filled liquid, and for a blissful moment she imagined she were once again on the beach of Barbados, feeling the shifting sand beneath her slippers.

Perhaps she'd spent too long imagining a better life,

waiting first for her father to rescue her from the fate of ending up a mistress of one of the surly sugar barons who journeyed to the West Indies in search of riches, and then for Lord Braunschweig to sweep her away into one of the fairytale stories she savored.

Somehow she'd forgotten that fairytales were not real.

Chapter Nineteen

S he was Loretta Van Lochen.

She'd never mentioned it to Miles.

Why wouldn't she be her? She was so smart, so clever, so amusing.

No wonder she hadn't wanted money.

She'd confided in Lord Braunschweig, yet she hadn't told him. The thought wounded him, more than he would have thought possible.

He shook his head. If only he hadn't been so emphatic in his criticisms of the other man.

Music sounded. A woman was singing. He glanced over. He knew that voice. He knew that woman.

Miles cursed himself for slandering the baron. The man was nothing what he'd pictured him to be. He was perhaps Miles's age, not the tottering old man he'd feared. He was even, Miles was forced to admit, attractive in his own way. Nothing about him was off-putting. He hadn't even needed to be forced to acknowledge Veronique.

Likely some reasonable excuse, the type Veronique had insisted on, had hindered him.

She would be fine.

He wandered to the punch section. He recognized various female acquaintances. He tried to concentrate on the conversation.

He didn't want her to be with Lord Braunschweig. He wanted her for himself. The thought was unbidden, but true.

He wished it were yesterday. He wished they were still traveling together. Even when they'd been in a crowded carriage, even when they hadn't actually been speaking, he'd still hoped that once she met Lord Braunschweig, she might choose him instead.

The thought was balderdash.

"My dear Lord Worthing," a woman in an alto voice said. "What brings you to Yorkshire? I wasn't aware this county sufficed in excitement for you."

"Mrs. Parker." He gave the widow a light bow, and she dipped into an elegant curtsy.

This was not the first time they'd met.

Her eyes sparkled. "You've made this ball much more interesting by your presence."

"Oh, I wouldn't say that." He glanced again in Veronique's direction, but she was obscured by a group of young debutantes who bounced about the ballroom with up tempo music.

"You must regale me with your stories." She leaned toward him. "You can start by fetching me a drink."

"Naturally." He moved to the punch table and obtained two glasses of negus. He handed her a glass and sipped his own. The colors were pleasing to look at, but it lacked the sharp alcohol taste he found he craved.

She gave him another smile, but he struggled to think of anything to say to her.

"You haven't complimented me on my dress yet," she said. "Or perhaps you require me to twirl before you?"

"Oh, it's very nice," he said.

And it was. It was white, so it almost looked like she could be a Greek Goddess from the new British Museum. Well, if Greek Goddesses had blonde hair and wore diamond necklaces.

Her eyes sparkled again. "You seem distracted."

"Forgive me. My—er—ankle hurts." It wasn't his ankle. It was more in the chest direction, more in the heart area.

"Then let's speak," she said.

"Yes." He frowned. "Do you by any chance know Lord Braunschweig?"

So many people had arrived from the continent after the war, and Miles had not kept track of all of them.

"I hope you're not trying to thrust me on him. He's far too dull. Even if he is very good looking. I suppose the man is allowed to have some advantage to comfort him with the fact that he's from Prussia."

"He's Austrian, I believe."

"Then the man has no excuses," Mrs. Parker said.

"Why isn't he married yet?"

She laughed. "I would think you of all men would understand why men choose not to marry."

"He is with many women?"

"Have you seen him? Those features are so elegantly placed." She sighed. "It's a pity the man's so poor."

"Is he?"

"He's from the continent, my dear. When are they are not? Place destroyed by Bonaparte I believe. Some such tragic story." She leaned closer. "Though between you and me, who is to say he's an actual baron? I never heard of him before the war. He certainly wasn't educated in England. There must be a reason no fathers have permitted their daughters to marry him beyond the fact foreigners are often seen as a last resort. One never knows which European country will implode next."

Lord Worthing tried to concentrate on the widow's conversation, but he soon made his excuses and went outside. He thought he saw the Fitzroys inside, hanging near their mama, given the older woman's remarkable likeness to them. Perhaps their parents deemed Yorkshire sufficiently tame for them.

The night was still, devoid now of the rumble of carriage wheels. The guests had halted their exploration of the garden in favor of Lady Mulborne's ample supply of alcohol and her good taste in music. Her husband may have passed on, but Lady Mulborne remained an excellent hostess and showed no desire of isolating herself.

He sat down on the steps and gazed into the night, his heart too heavy for someone who'd safely delivered a woman to her fiancé and assured himself more years of rakish bachelorhood.

A figure strode nearer him.

Miss Haskett.

He sighed. "I hope you do not intend to compromise me again."

She shook her head. "I apologize for that. I did not realize you were otherwise engaged."

"Saw me as an opportunity?"

"Would you blame me? I was tired of being forced to take long cross country trips."

He frowned. "I'm no good."

She laughed. "I know that—now."

"Oh."

"Besides, one doesn't need to be too clever to know you're in love with that woman you were traveling with."

He blinked.

I love Veronique.

The thought soared through his mind.

He shook his head. It couldn't be true. He wasn't the type to fall in love. He was in control of his emotions. He wasn't the type to be impulsive. But he loved her all the same.

"I love her," he said, his voice rough.

Miss Haskett eyed him strangely.

"Forgive me." He despised he was telling this woman that. He should be telling Veronique. He should be clasping her in his arms and declaring his passion to her—forever and ever and ever.

He ascended the steps. He needed to find her.

Chapter Twenty

"Dancing was a mistake," Lord Braunschweig said. "The process can be difficult."

"Oh." Her cheeks warmed.

"And it wouldn't do for people to pay too much attention to you," he said.

Veronique frowned. "Why not?"

She despised that her voice faltered.

He lifted her arm. "Your skin is not as white as the other women. They'll be curious soon."

"Some people asked me if I had Spanish blood," she admitted.

"I hope you told them yes."

Veronique blinked.

"Even being a bloody Spaniard is an improvement on your heritage." He smiled. "Surely I need not explain that to you?"

She gave him her loftiest frown, trying to avoid dwelling on the fact she'd just met the man whom she'd spent the past two years dreaming of marrying and she should not be occupying her first ten minutes of conversation with him with showcasing her surliest scowls.

This had all been a mistake.

She didn't know Lord Braunschweig any better than she knew the elegantly dressed *ton* members who cast curious looks at her.

Lord Worthing had been completely, utterly, correct.

She never should have insisted on marrying a man she'd never met.

She'd been foolish to insist he elope with her in Scotland, and she should have been thankful that Lord Braunschweig had shown too much sense to make an appearance.

She certainly should never have left the castle to make her own way to him.

She'd always assumed herself to be intelligent.

She turned, trying to seek out Lord Worthing.

She needed to speak with him.

She glanced toward Lord Worthing. The last time she'd seen him he'd been surrounded by finely attired women. Likely they spoke with the same rounded vowels he used, and their skin were of the peaches-and-cream variety every English poet lauded.

They were sweet girls in white muslin dresses. They didn't spend their time writing risqué romances. Their attention was occupied in painting water colors of their parents' exquisite gardens and in practicing the pianoforte. The largest conundrum they'd likely faced today was selecting their gown.

Lord Worthing should be with someone like that. Someone appropriate who would never cause a scandal that might hamper his career, and who would never give journalists cause to wonder on anything except their consistently exquisite taste.

And perhaps Lord Braunschweig also should marry someone similar.

What was she thinking, rushing after a man? If he'd cared for her, even a portion of how she'd cared for him, he would have shown up. He wouldn't have stopped at a house party, eager for a reason to halt the uncomfortable carriage ride.

He wouldn't have allowed her to stand shivering in a cold chapel with a disapproving vicar while wearing a wedding dress. He hadn't even apologized to her.

He was no longer a fantasy, his name no longer a beacon of hope. He was real.

He was handsome and perhaps intelligent, but he wasn't Lord Worthing.

Somehow that fact mattered a great deal.

"Let's go outside," Lord Braunschweig said quickly.

Veronique hesitated, but she would need to discuss her doubts with him. No one should overhear their conversation.

They strode from the ballroom, following a crowd of people outside. He led her around the corner of the manor house.

It was now dark, but stars sparkled above. Torches flickered light over the facade of the home.

"It's quite nice here," she said.

"Yes," Lord Braunschweig said. "It's an old house. You wouldn't know about them. It even has a medieval maze."

"How interesting," Veronique said.

"Not really." Lord Braunschweig strode toward the maze, and Veronique followed him. "Other mazes are even grander. More complex. I'll show you them."

She blinked. For a moment she'd forgotten they'd planned to wed.

"We can marry soon," Lord Braunschweig said. "Then fewer people will be upset not to receive invitations."

"And why could we not have more people attend?" Her voice wobbled. She'd been happy to plan with him to marry in the chapel. The privacy had seemed romantic to her. But perhaps the man had another reason for a small ceremony, one that did not involve love and intimacy.

"My dear," Lord Braunschweig said. "I wouldn't want you to have to deal with people's questions about your heritage."

She drew her eyebrows together.

"Ach, you were very brave coming here tonight, just to see me," Lord Braunschweig said, stepping close to her. "But I wouldn't want people to have the chance to scrutinize you too closely."

Her spine coiled, and tension shot through her body, as if he'd turned her limbs to wood.

He stepped nearer her, and his eyes seemed to soften. Perhaps he was fond of her in his way. He had written her many letters...

"I'll take you to my home. You'll be safe there." He rubbed a thick finger over her cheek. "You can continue writing your books."

It was what she'd always wanted.

But instead of leaping into his arms, uncertainty rushed through her. She tried to envision herself at his townhome. She was used to being alone, accustomed even to not attending balls, but she didn't want that for herself anymore.

And yet...

She didn't want to appear in Scotland without a

husband on her arm. She didn't want her father and
stepmother to give her smug glances and give predictable
laments.

She didn't need to experience that. She had Lord
Braunschweig.

"Come here." He reached his hand toward her, and she
hesitated, gazing at the short, stubby fingers. "I didn't get a
ring, but I'm sure we are beyond such trivialities."

Who needs a ring when you have access to my income?

The thought came unbidden into her mind. It couldn't
be true—could it?

She'd needed her brother Arthur to open a bank
account for her. She could only imagine it would be
transferred to her husband after her marriage. Even if she
was seen as capable of producing the income, she was not
seen as capable of controlling it.

Hadn't Lord Braunschweig mentioned in his letters his
exasperation with the poor agriculture that had harmed
his properties in Austria and Britain?

"Perhaps we shouldn't marry." Her heartbeat
quickened, as if aware of the enormity of what she'd just
said.

Lord Braunschweig paused. "I must have misheard."

"You didn't." She swallowed hard, as if the action
might soothe her speeding heart. "I should leave."

"You're too late."

"The ball is still going on."

His clasped about her wrist. "You're not going
anywhere."

She stepped back. For the first time she was aware they
were far from the others. It had seemed like a good idea
to have their conversation in private, away from the titters

and stares of the society women who swished about in their empire cut gowns and turbans.

She gave a desperate sort of laugh, and the man's other hand clapped around her mouth.

"You don't tell me no," Lord Braunschweig said.

"I—" The sound came out muffled, and he shuffled her over the neatly trimmed grass. She stumbled over flowers, and her nostrils flared.

"You should have been beside yourself with joy that I condescended to marry you." Lord Braunschweig's voice was firm. "You're so lowly born. You think that because your stepbrother is a duke, no one can tell you're colored?"

He pushed her forward, and her hands fell into thick bushes.

Lord Braunschweig laughed. "This way, idiot."

Her throat dried. She tried to call out, but he kept his hand over her mouth, and she felt only his gloved hands.

The man had appeared so proper. Even dull.

"We're going to be protected here." He yanked her forward, and tears prickled her eyes. They wound through the maze, and Veronique tried to remember the direction they'd taken in case she might run away.

But she couldn't run away.

He pushed her to the ground and lay on top of her, his hands moving roughly over her dress, which must be now stained by the grass and dirt.

I was a fool.

She'd allowed herself to believe in romance, in hope, in love.

But she'd only forced Lord Worthing to accompany her to find a man wholly undeserving of her praise.

Tears prickled her eyes, and in the next moment she

felt rough lips against hers and stubby hands grasping her bosom.

She struggled free as Lord Braunschweig concentrated on sucking her neck. "Help! Help!"

He pulled her back toward him, and turned her face down against the dirt and gravel. "Be quiet, woman."

*

Veronique had been gone for too long.

Some people stepped outside, and Miles peered at the bored expressions of the *ton*, any joy from the party evaporating as they waited for their coaches in the cool night breeze.

A woman shrieked, and Miles shivered.

The voice came from the maze.

It was unlikely the woman had stumbled against a bear, and Miles's fists curled in anger against the men of his class.

He scowled and headed toward the maze.

Where on earth was Veronique? He called her name as he strode over the lawn. People stared at him as he trampled over flowers and grass blades with ever firmer strides.

"Veronique!" he shouted again.

She must be inside the maze.

Miles had given her tepid warnings, stated his concerns politely, but when she'd needed him the most, he'd left her to choose on her own.

He hadn't given her the option of choosing him.

Lord Worthing rushed through the maze. In the past he'd found the smell of the yew trees pleasant. He'd once felt a source of pride at his English heritage. He'd always liked the use of geometry for leisure purposes.

He found nothing less amusing now.

These mazes seemed to have been built on the whim of medieval men with the same cunning and contempt for others which had led them to boil people alive who'd dared to adhere to a slightly different theological allegiance.

He padded through the maze, conscious of the intricate paths that led only to dead ends. The dark light did not help him as he sought to remember his way. He took silent notes to himself. Five paces to the right, and then when stopped by the thick wall of greenery, no less harmful despite its pristine, exquisite appearance, he turned.

"Veronique," he called out. "Where are you?"

"Miles?" Her voice came softly.

Blast.

He had to find her.

He climbed on top of the maze, pulling himself over the prickly bushes and crawled over them. His knees sank into the thorny undergrowth, but he kept crawling, thanking the centuries and the gardeners for allowing the bushes to grow so thick.

The branches tore the palms of his hands, but he was evading the dead ends he'd so frequently found when proceeding on foot through the designated paths designed precisely to get people lost.

Finally he saw them.

"Halt!" he shouted.

Lord Braunschweig didn't pause. His hands pulled up Veronique's dress. Any moment now—

Miles jumped.

As far as jumps went, this was inelegant.

He didn't land on Lord Braunschweig, even though the man deserved to be crushed to the ground. He stumbled up and glared at the baron.

"What is going on?" Miles shouted, though he didn't need to ask.

Lord Braunschweig's actions were obvious. He was about to violate the dearest woman in the world, judging from the lady's torn attire.

"Go away," Lord Braunschweig muttered. "This woman is mine."

"She's not," Miles said, conscious that his voice was icy cold.

"She's a whore."

Miles stiffened at the words and then yanked Lord Braunschweig up. "You apologize."

"I can't," Lord Braunschweig said. "Not when I'm right. She's a little colored girl. And you know the filth she writes?"

Lord Worthing blinked, and Lord Braunschweig smiled.

Whack.

Miles struck Lord Braunschweig in the face. He toppled over, and Miles rushed to help Veronique up.

Chapter Twenty-one

S he blinked up at the figure, but she knew it was Miles. It could only be him. Relief eased through her.

She heard Lord Braunschweig's footsteps, suitably loud for his long frame, thud down the path.

Miles glanced behind him. "I will deal with him later."

A cool breeze still brushed through the air, and floral scent still filled her nostrils. The sound of the music still infused the air.

She should be fine, but her body shivered.

"You poor thing," Miles said. "I'm so sorry."

"It's not your fault," she said. "I should have listened. I should never have come here."

She looked at the ground. She didn't want to see Miles's disappointment. He'd seen how Lord Braunschweig had touched her. He'd seen his stubby hands over her. He'd... She pulled up her bodice, unsure exactly what he'd seen.

Shame warmed her face. "I didn't mean—"

"I suppose he couldn't wait until the wedding night." The man looked down at the ground. It was more a question than a statement.

She closed her eyes tightly. "We're not getting married."

She pulled her arms together.

She'd almost whispered the statement, but the words seemed to roar in the still night. She closed her eyes, unwilling to see Lord Worthing's expression changed.

He'd done so much to get her here. Maybe he'd been unwilling at first, but he'd defended her, protected her.

They'd determined the only way to avoid getting married was for her to wed Lord Braunschweig. If she refused to marry him, after they'd spent even more time together, after they'd spent nights sleeping in the same room, same barn, conscious the other person was close by...

She didn't want to look at Lord Worthing. The man might think—

"I should rise." She didn't want to. She didn't want anyone to see her. She smoothed the lovely dress Lord Worthing had gotten her, conscious that leaves and flowers were still pressed against the sumptuous fabric.

She thought of the care she'd taken to dress for this evening, and shame filled her once again. If only she'd known. But she had, hadn't she? She'd been warned. Lord Worthing had warned her.

"I'm sorry I didn't listen to you," she said.

Lord Worthing extended his hand. "Come on, let's get you cleaned up."

She shivered at his firm touch, so reassuring, contrasting so much to the clammy, forceful fingers of

Lord Braunschweig. "I spent two years yearning to meet him, counting the days until I could."

She shook her head and then realizing that more tendrils were falling from her coiffure than was appropriate, she pinned back her curls. She must look a state. "I suppose you'll have to tell my family now. I suppose I should be locked up for the rest of my life."

"I don't think you would find being locked up favorable," Lord Worthing said. "We wouldn't want you to destroy any sheets again."

She tried to laugh, but it was so difficult. Her heart still thumped, and if she closed her eyes, she could still imagine the feel of Lord Braunschweig on top of her. "I—"

"You don't have to speak now," Lord Worthing said calmly. "I'm here, and you're safe."

She rose and took his hand. They strode through the maze. He still grasped her fingers, and she had no desire to let go.

"I'm so sorry," she said mournfully, her voice wobbling, distracted by the feel of his hand against hers. She stared straight ahead of her, and willed her heart to calm. "What was I thinking?"

She felt Lord Worthing fixing his gaze on her, and she shivered under his observation.

She stepped away, because the urge to step toward him, to feel his warm arms about her was too tempting.

She'd already changed his life too much, forcing him to accompany her.

Tears prickled her eyes, and she gazed down at her dress.

This was supposed to be her perfect evening. The meeting with Lord Braunschweig should have been even nicer than the one she'd planned. After all, they hadn't met in a drafty chapel constructed several centuries ago.

The music still trickled from the windows of the manor house, merging with laughter and chatter.

She should be just as happy.

After two years of longing to meet Lord Braunschweig, she finally had. This should have been the happiest day of her life.

She shivered and wrapped her shawl more tightly around her. The ornate lace, so pretty in its case, dug into her skin.

When they'd first met, Lord Worthing had asked if he might kiss her. He hadn't insisted. He in no way deserved the horrible reputation she was certain her stepmother would be all too happy to give him were he to refuse.

And yet because of an action which she'd taken part in, his life, everything he cared about would be destroyed.

"I'm glad you won't marry him," Lord Worthing said.

"Oh."

"I can't be standing about him to tackle him whenever he decides to approach you all my life."

She almost laughed. "I thought this whole time, for so many years—I thought he cared about me. This is all my fault, and now you'll feel pressured by my parents to marry me. I won't let that happen, please don't worry. I have the funds, you don't need to be beholden to me."

"You should have told me who you were," Lord Worthing said.

"I know. Forgive me."

"I feel foolish. All that time I spoke of Loretta Van Lochen..."

She shook her head. "You were doing your job. And I—I wanted to keep mine."

"Would that go away if people knew who you are?" Lord Worthing asked gently.

She nodded, and her stomach hurt at the thought that so despicable a man as Lord Braunschweig knew her deepest secret.

"I won't tell anyone," Lord Worthing said.

"Thank you. I was overly romantic," she said. "Just like you said.

"I wouldn't want you to change."

"You told me romance was a foolish concept, one that you couldn't believe in."

"I believe in it now," he said, his voice warm and soothing.

"Oh," she repeated, cognizant that her response was nonsensical.

A masculine scent of pine needles and cotton, brandy and cedar, wrapped about her, and her heart beat rapidly against a foreign chest.

Her knees wobbled, as if urging her to succumb to the blissful sensation of being in Lord Worthing's arms. It would be so easy to go along with him, to agree with him that Lord Braunschweig was less than ideal, and to pretend ignorance of the pressure he would come under to marry her himself.

She stiffened. Was this what he intended? Perhaps he might even feign happiness on the matter to best assure her this was the correct thing to do. Men could have an overly developed sense of honor; reading heroic tales as children might have a too dramatic impact on them.

She pushed away from him, refusing to ponder the blissful sensation of pressing her fingers against his sturdy chest. "I might buy a cottage on the coast somewhere."

"Is that what you desire?"

"Yes. With a nice large garden. I've—I've always wanted it." This wasn't a lie. She'd just always imagined she would be living with somebody she cared about. She'd imagined that somebody might not mind who her grandmother was.

"It will be splendid," she chirped, moving away from Lord Worthing. She stepped into the garden and looked at the flowers. She stroked a petal impulsively. "Th-this is pretty. I'll have to have these."

"I see."

She turned around. "In my garden. At my house. Where I'll be very h—"

Arms pulled her toward him, and in the next moment Lord Worthing's lips were on hers. Heaven could not be as blissful as this.

"But—"

"I don't want you to speak of any garden," Lord Worthing whispered. "Unless it's the one at the home where we're living together."

Her eyes widened. "But—"

"You're marrying me."

"But you needn't. I can take care of—"

"Yourself," Lord Worthing finished. "So you've told me before."

"I rescued you," Veronique reminded him.

"And you'll just have to keep on doing that," Lord Worthing said, before taking her into his arms once again.

She wanted to tell him to stop. But he feathered kisses on her face, tracing the line from her cheek to her neck. His kisses grew warmer, wetter, and when he sucked on her thin flesh, she was certain nothing in the world was more ridiculous than the prospect of pushing him away from her.

He was everything in the world. And if he wanted to be near her, she would let him.

It wasn't the first time he'd kissed her, and her lips sought his again eagerly. Reason was something for her mind, she decided.

The world swayed, but then he withdrew from her arms. His gaze was more solemn.

Oh.

He'd seen reason.

She tried to smile. She wouldn't let him think her unhappy for even a second. He deserved to be happy. He didn't need to worry about her feelings.

"My dear Veronique." His voice, normally so strong, wobbled.

Her heart tumbled down forward

And then she blinked, because Miles lowered.

He was—kneeling before her.

"Veronique Daventry," he said. "Will you do me the tremendous honor of becoming my wife?"

Her heart stopped. Joy surged through her.

"Veronique?" he asked, more uncertainly. "I know you might not see me in that way, but—"

"I do," she said, pulling him up from the ground and wrapping her arms about him.

He drew his hand through her hair, seeming to find joy in twirling his fingers through her now loose curls.

The stars sparkled above, clear in the countryside, and Veronique allowed Miles's words to sweep over her.

The manor house seemed to glow behind them, flickering torches illuminating the white stone with its facades of Greek and Roman mythology.

It was so different from Barbados.

No palm trees loomed above her, and the scent of the ocean was replaced with that of dozens of flowers.

She blinked, half-expecting to wake up and find she was back in Massachusetts, scribbling her novels while her stepsisters attended the balls she longed to join.

The other half of her expected to wake in Barbados, defending herself from the words of sailors and fortune makers, alternatively demeaning her and intent on conquering her oriental charm. As if Barbados, in the Caribbean, had anything to do with the orient.

But she was still here, in this magnificent maze, with Miles.

The kisses grew stronger, deeper, until she pulsated with desire. How could something she'd never felt before, except with him, feel like the strongest force in the world?

"You drive me wild," Miles said, between long, desperate kisses. "When I thought you might marry Lord Braunschweig..."

"You always thought that," Veronique reminded him.

He stroked her hair. "I'd started to hope you wouldn't."

"Even though you adore your freedom?"

He gave a short laugh. "Just a nicer word for boredom."

He'd caused her heart to hammer when she'd first met him, had caused her to lose all sense of propriety from the very beginning. She knew she should be telling him to wait. That was the proper thing to do. But instead she succumbed to the sensation of his soothing strokes over her skin.

Chapter
Twenty-two

It had been dashed improper to bring her here. He abhorred Lord Braunschweig.

Veronique wasn't an opera singer, wasn't an actress, wasn't a woman tired of her husband and eager for adventure—Veronique was the most wonderful woman in the world.

Standing beside her waiting for the coach to queue in any sort of appropriate manner would be agony.

He'd experienced enough distress at the ball. Bringing her here, so she could meet someone else.

He shook his head.

No. She was his, and he was going to claim her.

They strolled the yew maze. It had been here for centuries, older than the current, modern additions of the manor house. The hedges were thick and stretched eight feet from the ground, hiding the manor house.

The stars still peaked over them, and moonlight highlighted Veronique's lovely figure.

His heartbeat quickened, and he clasped her fingers in his. Her vanilla scent mingled with that of the yew trees, and his head swirled. Longing rushed through him, and he pulled her toward him, as if to assure him of her presence.

Their feet crunched over the gravel, and the music grew increasingly faint.

"My darling." His voice thickened.

He'd been so worried all evening that she might marry Lord Braunschweig. He should have been relieved that he could resume his carefree life, but all he'd felt was worry he'd never see her again.

She knew him better than anyone else.

And though once that fact might have worried him, instead he felt only relief.

His lips hovered inches from hers, and he rested his hands on her hips. Gaps between them were best narrowed. Her body seemed to melt against his, and he was conscious of all manner of slender curves and soft skin.

Kissing was a skill he prided himself in. But somehow his kisses had never felt so all-consuming before. Desire surged through him, and he crushed her against him, pressing her bodice to his chest.

Air seemed far less interesting compared to tasting her.

"Perhaps we should go back," he said, almost as a plea.

Perhaps if they left right now, he could leave her with her maidenhood still protected. Every moment alone with her was dangerous.

"Or we could stay," Veronique said after a pause.

"I don't think I can restrain myself."

She stepped nearer him, and her voice was low. "Perhaps you needn't."

He took her shawl and laid it on the ground. "I'm going to make use of your practicality."

"That wasn't why I brought the shawl," she murmured.

"Tell me to stop."

She didn't.

"It's fine," he said more seriously. "If you really would rather move to your cottage near the sea. I know you can take care of yourself."

"I don't want to," she whispered.

She lay down on the shawl, and Miles settled beside her. They were in darkness, but he'd long ago memorized the placement of the delicate features of her face and the curves of her body, visible even when swathed in dusty attire.

He flung his tailcoat off, and then more slowly unwound his cravat. She touched the coarse, hastily unfolded linen with reverence.

He brushed his fingers over her bosom, tracing them with wonder. Then his lips moved from her lips to her neck to her bosom. Every one of his nerve endings sang as he explored new, wondrous parts of her body.

"Veronique," he murmured, saying her name as one might utter a prayer. Wonder emanated through his voice.

His heart thudded beneath his ribs, as if at any moment prepared to pound an Italian symphony.

The scent of grass and flowers and...Veronique filled his nostrils, causing his head to swirl with greater force than any alcohol heavy concoction.

Veronique moaned, and Miles concentrated on bringing more delightful sounds from her. Her curves beckoned him, and he pulled her toward him. Her long skirt pressed against his trousers, and he raised the hem, cursing whomever had invented pantalettes.

Anything that separated them, even linen, seemed an enemy worthier of scorn than anything Bonaparte had ever done.

She moved, winding her legs about him. She echoed his movement, and Miles became more conscious of the need to touch his lips against more skin. He pulled her pantalettes off and ran his fingers over her long legs. He wanted to memorize every inch of her.

*

Desire rushed through her. Even though desire was nothing she'd ever considered before, it seemed now like the largest force of anything else in the world: greater than hunger, thirst or any yearning for protection from the icy cold wind that billowed over them. Desire was everything. Miles was everything, and he might actually be hers.

Her heartbeat fluttered. It beat a new rhythm, a new symphony. Something that if anyone could record would surely compete with the likes of Beethoven. His fingers, long and firm, roamed over her with expertise, and every skin cell in her body seemed to wake up at his mere presence.

Energy surged through her and made her back arch up to him. Her legs seemed to naturally tangle with his, pulling him closer to her. The one thing she was absolutely certain of now, even though her mind seemed to have completely floated away, flying through the heavens themselves, was that Miles needed to be right beside her, right on top of her.

Even an inch apart from him would equal the vastness between the coasts of the Atlantic Ocean.

"You are wonderful." Miles's voice was warm, sultry,

and comforting. He stroked his fingers through her hair, which had now become undone somewhere after she'd hit the earth.

His fingers twirled her locks, naturally curly, with something that seemed very like reverence. He didn't wonder at the thickness of each strand, marveling at how it managed to spring up so quickly, and comparing it unfavorably with his own.

He moved his finger up to her face, as if memorizing the exact shape of her upturned nose was as important to him as any cricket match.

"I need you," he said.

She nodded. She needed him too.

He moved his lips to hers, and in the next moment they were back where they had been in the chapel. She was being transported to the heavens themselves, to Atlantis, to ancient Greece, to every magnificent place in this world and beyond.

His lips ran over hers, moving to the curve of her neck and the place where it met her shoulders.

And everything that she knew of him. Miles managed to be adventurous, exciting, moving. But now as he held her pressed against his chest, he seemed only filled with reverence. He brushed his hands against her, his strokes tender, and even though she was lying in a maze, some garden contraption built centuries ago to amuse bored medieval aristocrats, in his arms she only felt safe.

The stars and the moon lit his face. Not very well, but she'd long ago memorized the exact shade of his skin, and the multitude of laughs and smiles he was so prone to giving her. Moonlight illuminated the contours of his chiseled features and he looked every bit as magnificent as any Greek or Roman statue Lady Alfriston might manage to pull from the ground triumphantly. He was everything.

"I need you," he said. "I don't understand it. I don't need anyone, but I sure as hell need you."

"I feel the same. If you're insane, you're not the only one."

"The word we use here is mad." He smoothed the curve of her cheek beneath his fingers. "I should get you inside. Being here outside, with you, makes me long for things, desire things so utterly and completely..."

"What would you want to do?"

"Besides haul you over my shoulder straight back across the Scottish border to marry you?"

"Yes," she said.

She wasn't naïve. One didn't become a writer of penny dreadfuls without some knowledge of passion. All her information, though, derived from the whispers and giggles of servants, and the more flowery prose of her contemporaries.

"I desire you as well," she said.

"You mustn't say that. I might devour you."

"I am yours." She knew that was true. No matter what happened, she would always be his. She didn't need a marriage certificate to tell her that.

"My darling." He kissed her again, but this time with even greater force that sent pleasure coiling through her body with more vigor than any waterfall.

Her toes curled, and her fingers clutched him. She was his. She would always be his.

No doubt the vicar would be upset at how she was acting. Likely her parents would be disappointed. But the only thing in the world that mattered to her was the feel of his kiss against her lips as he pulled her closer to him.

Miles lay next to her, and she was aware of long muscular limbs pressed against hers. He glided his hands skillfully over her body, and he lowered her bodice.

He kissed her again, so very deeply, and she was certain he would feel her heartbeat thump against his.

Suddenly she was no longer cold, even though the sun had long since set, and they had likely not been transported to the warm sunny Caribbean, but she was no longer cold. She felt his hardness pressed against her hip. She grew accustomed to the feel of it against her, as he continued to stroke his hand through her hair.

No matter that her hair was not straight. She kissed him with more force, and desire swelled through her. When Miles lowered his mouth to her neck, moving lasciviously toward the edge of her bodice, she moved her hands over his chest and unbuttoned his frock jacket. She wasn't sure of the exact procedure, but she was absolutely certain that fewer clothes on Miles could only be an advantage. The mere touch of his skin seemed to warm her. Any fabric was an unwelcome barrier.

She pulled him nearer. The only thing that mattered was the feel of him, and when he pulled down her bodice and then unfastened her corset, she laughed with him at his delight.

He moved his hands lightly over her bosom, and she had the vague sense she was moaning. Miles did not seem to mind that she was completely inarticulate. For a moment he pulled away from her and unbuttoned the flap of his trousers.

"It was getting a bit uncomfortable," he said and grinned.

She smiled back, not quite knowing what he meant,

but in the next moment he placed her hand over his hardness.

She stared at him even though it was dark and she could not quite see his features, aware that everything in her life was changing. She couldn't be happier. He moved his hand up her dress and she scarcely had a moment to consider the size of his hardness. He continued to kiss her body, eagerly claiming each new inch that he exposed as he undressed her.

He moved his wet lips over her legs. "So long."

"Oh?"

He pulled her toward him, cupping her bottom, and she wrapped her hands around his neck and gazed at the stars as they twinkled above like jewels.

His lips moved toward the most intimate portion of her body. She'd heard of men exploring this region, but it seemed too private. He couldn't possibly be venturing there.

The next moment was bliss.

Pleasure swept through her. His tongue was clearly the most magnificent thing in the world, and it glided over her.

She could feel him.

She moved her fingers tentatively to his length feeling it expand still further.

He moaned and then wrapped his arms around her, undressing, sliding her dress down. He brushed his lips against her neck, and he angled his hardness against her center. Energy tightened within her.

She knew the basic procedure, but she'd never imagined it could feel so nice.

Her heart beat quickly, and she heard him shudder as he pressed further into her. At first the sensation felt somewhat strange, and she shivered, realizing how unnatural their positions were, lying half-undressed in this maze. But then Miles began to move, and the world swirled. His hands once again swept over her, and he kissed her

A new strange craving rushed through her, and she didn't know whether she desired release or if she wanted the sensation to go on forever.

Miles had seemed calm before, but his breath became quicker, more uneven, and she felt pride that she was bringing him to this reaction.

He moved deeper into her, filling her completely.

She was his.

She would always be.

She succumbed to the sensation of his fingers against hers, led on by this new desire.

"I cannot resist any longer," he said.

"Then don't."

Miles started to relinquish control. He wrapped his strong muscular arms around her, and his thrusts grew deeper, harder, rocking her very soul.

And then with a cry he pulled out quickly. She wondered if she'd done something wrong, but he spilled his seed on the grass.

"My darling." He flung himself beside her, wrapping her in his arms, his breath still heavy and uneven.

The smell of the seed mingled with that of the flowers and bushes in the maze.

"Now for you," he said.

"Me?" She'd rather assumed the action to be over, but he moved his hands over her legs, once again entering her center with them.

His tongue was more interested in her bosom, and pleasure shot through her when he thrust his fingers deeply into her body and moved them with an expert rapidity.

Energy coursed through her.

She found herself arching her back toward him, and waves of pleasure shot through her. Her breath grew uneven, and she found herself pushing her body against his fingers, conscious of his lips continuing to mark her.

Then her insides tensed in pleasure, and she shuddered on the ground, and he pulled her into a longer, messy embrace as she fought to catch her breath.

"I love you," he said, and her heart continued to soar.

Chapter
Twenty-three

A twig snapped, and Veronique stiffened. She tilted her
ear in the direction of the sound. Miles continued to
stroke her hair, seeming more occupied with the feel of her
tresses against the palm of his hand than with whatever
was distracting her.

Someone was here. Veronique had never thought
twigs frightening, but now her spine coiled with fear at the
sheer sound of a fallen branch cracking.

"I think we should go," Veronique said.

The music had stopped playing. It was quiet, except for
the sound of her beating heart.

She couldn't hear horses trot over the gravel, and she
couldn't hear people, stragglers from the party. No one
should be here now.

She lifted her torso and rose. The scent of the maze still
filled her nostrils, and the stars still twinkled above, but for
the first time she felt uneasy.

Miles stood up. He rested his hand against the curve of

her back. "It doesn't matter. It doesn't matter at all. Lady Montague herself can find us, and it won't matter."

"Truly?" Veronique asked.

"Truly," Miles said. "We're getting married, and I want to marry you soon."

They strolled through the maze. When they exited, she noticed a woman.

Veronique relaxed. She'd worried it had been Lord Braunschweig.

Still...The woman looked familiar, and Veronique recognized her as the woman on the coach. *Miss Haskett.* It wasn't good that anyone had seem them go out of the maze, so disheveled, so completely, utterly together. Veronique smoothed her dress hastily, removing the last blades of grass pressed against her dress.

She'd known the woman had been on the coach. That the woman had already seen them together. She also knew the woman was a governess. She wouldn't know her father or her stepmother.

Still it was odd that the woman seemed so amused.

Miles drew in his breath, and she glanced at him. His gaze remained on Miss Haskett, and he dropped hold of her hand, sending a shiver through her body as he stepped away.

Still... Tomorrow they could go back to Scotland and there they could elope, just as they almost had. In the chapel, with her family members, with this wonderful man whom she couldn't imagine being without.

The night was so beautiful. It might be darker now. The sun may have sunk, tilting to another side of the world, but it was still beautiful. The garden was still rich with floral scent, and the air was still warm. The musicians still played and the guests still danced when they entered the ballroom.

The hostess smiled at them from across the room.

"I'll be back soon," Miles said. "I have something important to do."

Veronique nodded, and he soon followed Lady Mulborne from the ballroom.

"Abandoned so early?" a voice said behind her, and Veronique swung around.

Miss Haskett smiled. "I had an extraordinary conversation with Lord Braunschweig."

Veronique swallowed hard. She wasn't afraid of people learning about her ancestors. She'd been proud of how she'd been raised, despite some people's propensity to describe people with her color skin in solely negative adjectives.

"I know everything about you," Miss Haskett said. "And soon so will everyone else."

"Do you mean to claim the reward?" Veronique's voice wobbled. "Because I can pay. More than the reward. I'm certain."

"Yes. I know about your writing hobby. Your offer is tempting. But I feel it is a duty to warn others about you." Miss Haskett's lips curled into a smirk. "I think people will find your colorful ancestry very relevant."

Villains in Veronique's experience, and what she tended to impart in her stories, were mustache-sporting men with a tendency to run their hands through their less than ideal facial hair while narrowing their eyes and uttering demeaning comments. The villains were often physically strong, and when they weren't that, they had the weapons to make up for their lack of muscular girth.

Veronique had never seen a villain like Miss Haskett.

A woman of perhaps her own age, a woman like her, who may not have experienced everything. Miss Haskett was perhaps a woman she would have liked to befriend, and yet more than anyone else in this great and wonderful world she had the ability to destroy everything.

She heard a noise, and she realized it was the sound of other people tittering in the room. The noise seemed to swell, perhaps helped by the excellent acoustics of the ballroom that clearly carried laughter just as easily as it carried arias.

Miss Haskett took a spoon and clanged it against a glass of negus.

No one heard.

She forced herself to think the lie, but it did nothing to calm the beating of her heart. She felt ridiculous in her gown.

She'd spent so long immersing herself in this world. She'd read so many books set in Europe. She'd thought perhaps since it was across the ocean and that the farmers there did not employ slaves, that she wouldn't experience the sneers and ill language that some people directed at her.

She wrapped her arms together, and then, conscious of gazes on her, returned them to her side. She didn't want to seem upset. But the mere action of standing seemed impossibly difficult, a feat equaled only by the best athletes.

"Ladies and gentlemen," Miss Haskett said. "I have an announcement to make. An imposter is among us."

The crowd murmured.

"I have discovered Loretta Van Lochen!"

Some people applauded, and Veronique felt a tinge of pride.

"Who is she?" some people cried out. "I want to meet her!"

"You shouldn't," Miss Haskett said. "She should not have been permitted to enter this ball...she is from Barbados. Her relatives were *slaves*."

More murmurs sounded, and Veronique fought the temptation to careen to the floor or run from the ballroom.

"Indeed," Miss Haskett said, and joy seemed to glisten from her eyes, the peculiar kind people seemed to experience when issuing the vilest gossip. "You've been reading books written by a woman devoid of any respectability."

"Are you certain?" one person mused. "She doesn't look like a negro."

"You are seeing her by candlelight," Miss Haskett said. "But I am certain that you will agree that in comparison my skin is paler. My nose is thinner, and I needed actual curling tongs for my hair. Hers is thick and unwieldy and decidedly inelegant."

"You're right," some people said.

"Where's Lady Mulborne?" another woman asked. "How did this woman get entry?"

"Likely from the conniving ways of her kind," Miss Haskett said.

"You shouldn't say that," one woman said. "What if she cries?"

Veronique supposed she should be grateful that someone had recognize that Miss Haskett's behavior was less than honorable, but the words only seemed to draw attention to the fact that she did very much want to cry.

Her eyes stung, as if the salty tears were already making their way down her cheeks. She blinked, and her nostrils flared in an unladylike manner as she tried to calm herself.

Her throat was dry, which was just as well, because she couldn't think of anything to say.

She glanced around her. Some people had stricken looks on their faces, and others whispered, likely to repeat Miss Haskett's comments to the crowd.

"The exit is that way," Miss Haskett smirked. "Perhaps you can ask one of the footmen to introduce you to one of your countrymen."

"I—"

"Though likely a footman is too important a servant to speak to a *negro*."

Veronique knew she was supposed to do nothing. She was supposed to feel shame. She was supposed to—at the very most rush to the balcony, and more likely just collapse claiming heat stress.

But she wasn't going to start being a proper woman of the *ton* now. That had stopped when she'd climbed out of the castle window.

She wasn't going to wait for Miles to return and defend her honor.

She tightened her fists and strolled toward Miss Haskett, conscious of the rapidity with which Miss Haskett's eyebrows flew up.

"I'm not afraid of you," Veronique spoke slowly, just in case Miss Haskett had difficulty grasping her words. Intelligence did not seem to be one of the governess's few favorable traits.

"I doubt that."

"You are a governess, and I am a sister of a duke."

"Stepsister," Miss Haskett said, but her voice faltered somewhat.

Veronique smiled. "Do you really think that makes such a difference? It's the first time you've been allowed at such an occasion, isn't it?" She strode nearer her. "And you're not making a favorable impression. Clearly it was a mistake to invite you in. You're causing a *spectacle*."

"That's nonsense," Miss Haskett said. "You are—"

But the titters had begun again, and Veronique had the curious sensation the women were laughing at Miss Haskett, not her.

It brought her meager satisfaction, and she gritted her teeth.

"But your relatives were *slaves*."

"Only because the pale people first brought to do the work were incapable of doing anything well." Veronique tossed her hair. "I want the baron, and I'm certain he wants me."

"That's true." A deep voice she recognized sounded behind her, and she swung around. Her heartbeat thumped madly.

He held something between his fingers. Something that seemed to...sparkle, and Veronique's heart tightened as he strode nearer her.

"Sweetheart." Miles held up a sapphire and diamond ring, and a murmur undulated through the throng of people. "I've already asked you to marry me, but I want everyone to know that you're mine, forever and ever and ever." He took her hand in his and slid the ring over her finger. "I love you."

"Oh, darling, I love you too," Veronique exclaimed.

She was vaguely aware of some furious coughing and throat clearing from some onlookers, the sound lessened by the applause and shouting of felicitations by others, but mostly she was aware of the sensation of his lips pressing against hers.

There would be other balls, and other coarse comments. Of that Veronique was certain.

She didn't mind. Not too much at least. She had a greater grasp of life than any of these women did, who were as cloistered as nuns, and whose etiquette guides could not teach them right from wrong.

*

Happiness was a brilliant state.

Miles was married. The memory still caused him to beam.

Lady Mulborne had insisted Veronique and he stay at her manor house, some space being available after both Lord Braunschweig and the Fitzroys and their charges vacated quickly to an inn in Harrogate.

He'd been able to send a new letter to Diomhair Caisteal announcing Veronique's and his marriage.

Their relatives had written back with their congratulations, stating for some reason that they'd expected it all along and that the connection between Veronique and him had been palpable and their union utterly predictable.

"My publisher told me my services would no longer be needed," Veronique said. "He read the article in *Matchmaking for Wallflowers* about me. Men were complaining that their servant girls were reading a book written by a woman of ill-repute."

"I'm sorry, sweetheart."

She sighed. "They had warned me."

"Likely those same people would be delighted to meet you in person."

"Because of my stepbrothers' titles?"

"And because you are the cleverest, most enchanting woman in the world."

Veronique smiled.

His editor had sent him a similar edict for managing to have the story about Loretta Van Lochen be broken by a women's magazine. His editor had thought Miles could not claim ignorance of Loretta Van Lochen's identity, since he'd been married to the authoress.

"I wonder how *Matchmaking for Wallflowers* found out so quickly."

"Miss Haskett must have asked for the reward," Veronique said.

A thought occurred to him.

He shook his head. It was too unlikely.

He thought of everything he knew about *Matchmaking for Wallflowers*. He'd been proud to be highly regarded by them. He should have despised more how the magazine had hurt his family, had hurt so many members of the *ton*.

Miles leaped from his seat. "I'm going to Harrogate. I believe the Fitzroys are still staying there."

He took his horse and hastened to the castle. The butler was surprised when he demanded to see Miss Haskett, but she was soon ushered to him.

"You're the editor of *Matchmaking for Wallflowers*," he said.

Miss Haskett tilted her head. "I don't know what you're speaking about."

Miles neared her. "You know precisely what I'm speaking about. It's a very successful pamphlet."

Miss Haskett smiled. "It is, isn't it?"

"I always imagined it was run by a member of the *ton*. But I suppose it makes more sense that it was run by someone like you."

"Like me?" Indignation flashed in her eyes.

The thought couldn't ease his outrage at her—she'd hurt too many people over the years, but he possessed a modicum of pleasure that he was rattling her.

"You're a governess. Somebody close enough to high society that you would know just what happens at every ball."

She shrugged.

"Your charges likely share the gossip with you."

"Conversation. Not gossip." She raised her chin. "*Matchmaking for Wallflowers* provides a useful service to society. I'm sure there's no higher compliment than to be affiliated with it."

"I very much doubt that. And I know most people feel the same as I do." Miles scrutinized her.

She was so different from what he'd imagined the editor would be like. Her hair was not perfectly coiffed, and the color of her afternoon dress clashed with her hat. Even the ribbons she'd purchased from the haberdasher seemed chosen for their garishness.

"Why did you take on the role of arbitrator-in-chief of others?" Miles asked.

"They have so many advantages," Miss Haskett said. "Unlimited funds. They could do so well. If they'd only listen."

"Mm-hmm. It must be difficult to be a governess. So near the higher ranks in the home. Spending so much time with them, but never belonging."

Miss Haskett averted her gaze. Her already pale face had whitened further, and her freckles seemed to be intensified.

"I—I belong," she said, but her voice wobbled.

"We both know that's not true." Miles was never one

for putting servants in their place, but Miss Haskett's utter cruelty to so many of his acquaintances and friends riled him.

"You laughed at the Duke of Alfriston after his war injury."

Miss Haskett shrugged. "I only reported what people were saying. Amaryllis and Theodosia both thought he would be easy prey."

"You humiliated him."

"No more than others humiliated me." She tossed her hair. "Besides, I didn't write anything. I hired people to write for me."

"Like Lady Rockport."

"Precisely. You wouldn't believe how many bored members of the *ton* there are. Even some men contributed."

"I see."

"I gave many people a purpose."

"By demeaning others," he said, conscious his tone was still outraged, but seeing no point in masking it. "Why do you do it? For the coin?"

She gave a bitter laugh. "I'm not the only editor. I do what I can to survive. The Fitzroys think I should be honored simply to be able to spend time with their daughters. I saw my parents die penniless. I know the importance of money."

"I wish you had shown some compassion."

She shrugged. "Does it really matter what you think?"

"Well—"

"Because I'm not sure it does," she continued, and her eyes flashed, reminding him of the biting words she'd written. "Haven't you both been thrown from your positions?"

Miles stiffened. "I wish you good day, ma'am."

"No one wants to publish books by a woman with such a colorful past," Miss Haskett called after him.

Miles cringed at the manner in which she said "colorful," but it didn't matter. He'd seen the letters Veronique received from her readers, confused to learn she would no longer be published.

Miles would ensure she would keep on doing what she loved.

Chapter
Twenty-four

The road dipped, and Miles guided the curricle into a small valley as Veronique leaned against him. The large wheels of the carriage stretched to Veronique's elbows and carried them swiftly over the dry road, sweeping up the occasional wildflower in their path. Jays and chaffinches chirped soliloquies, the sound replaced by new birds.

White towers poked over thick leafy trees, and Veronique leaned forward, as if the action might make them arrive sooner.

"This is your home," Veronique breathed.

Miles turned his head, and she was once again struck by the man's handsomeness. There was a reason his face had graced the covers of so many magazines when he was a foreign correspondent. No wonder artists did not tire at depicting his chiseled features, experimenting only with the angle of his face and the choice between evening and day attire.

He placed his hand over hers, and warmth cascaded through her at his firm touch. He turned to her, and his eyes gleamed. "Our home, my darling."

She nodded. Words had never been things she'd needed to strive for. Everything except them had been a struggle. But now she was only conscious of the pitter-patter of her heart, which seemed intent on rivaling the sound of the horses' hooves stomping over the dirt lane.

They rode past apple and cherry orchards, and the glimpse of the white towers disappeared behind the new cascade of trees. Pink and white blossoms adorned ancient dark branches that stretched toward the heavens, and crimson roses curved from hedges.

"The garden is behind the estate," Miles said. "You'll love it."

Veronique nodded.

"The stables are in that direction." Miles waved authoritatively to their side. "And that—that is the house."

She turned to follow his hand, trying not to be distracted by the light that danced over the golden hair on his wrists.

The manor house was before her.

"Oh," she murmured.

It was not the first manor house she'd seen. She'd seen plenty of staid homes on their journey from Scotland, their gray and brick facades stained from the incessant rain. This was though the most beautiful.

"I would hope," he said, leaning toward her, "that you'll refrain from clambering from our bedroom window. The maids might worry if they see the bed stripped bare.

"Are they the only ones who would worry?"

He took her hand in his larger one. "I have learned there is no woman I would worry about less."

She blinked.

"But." His expression grew more serious, and for an instant she could imagine him older. The thought did not displease her. "I assure you I would miss you most dreadfully."

"Oh," she murmured.

She was conscious there were definitely more words in her vocabulary than that. She hadn't filled her books with one-syllable murmurings.

"I love you, Veronique," he said. "With all my heart and all my soul."

She allowed the words to wash over her. He'd whispered them to her before, but now before their future home, she allowed herself to envision a family.

"I would miss you if you ever left," he said solemnly.

She glanced down at her hands, noting the manner in which her ring sparkled and gleamed from her finger. "I won't."

It seemed so unlikely she'd ever met him. If it hadn't been for Lord Braunschweig, would she have begged her father to visit Britain? How close she had come to not meeting Miles at all, and when she had, she'd crept away from him, preferring sliding down a white sheet fluttering in the harsh wind than to the prospect of conversation over scones and chocolate with him.

The horses halted, and servants rushed from the door and scurried into a long row.

"Come," Miles said, taking her hand again. "Let me introduce you to the people in your new home."

Home.

All those years in Barbados and Massachusetts, aware of people's whispers, she'd never dared to dream of happiness for herself. Happiness had seemed a concept best relegated for the heroes and heroines she'd written about. But she was a heroine too: she'd been one all along.

She followed her husband onto the carefully raked gravel. Her feet crunched against the stones, and the sound echoed underneath the tall manor home. For a moment she hesitated, unsure what the servants might think when gossip reached them of her heritage, unsure how Miles might feel if the neighbors in similarly majestic homes hesitated to visit them.

"I love you," he repeated, his breath warm on her neck.

That was all that mattered, and she nodded, feeling her dark curls cascade down her back. Some of the servants widened their eyes. They would just have to get used to her, and she beamed as she felt the warm sun rays against her skin.

"I want to show you something," Miles said.

"I think you've already been successful at that."

He grinned. "Let's enter."

She stepped underneath the portico, staring at the perfectly carved stone.

"Allow me." Miles swept her into his arms and marched her into the manor house. Behind them the servants clapped, breaking their formality.

"Medieval custom," he murmured, his breath hot against her ear.

She tightened her hold against him, conscious of the firmness of his torso.

Goodness. He was her husband. He'd sleep beside her every night.

"Perhaps I should just show you to the bedroom," Miles murmured, still carrying her in his arms.

"I wouldn't complain."

He grinned. "First things first." He marched her

through the corridor, sweeping her past oriental vases and gilded frame paintings of idyllic scenes.

He came to another door, and grasped hold of the ornate knob, and pushed it open.

There were books.

Many, many books.

Leather tomes with gilded lettering sparkled before her, and he swung her around so quickly she squealed in delight.

"Welcome to your new home."

"It's amazing," she murmured.

Two large mahogany desks sat next to each other.

"We can work here," Miles said.

Veronique smiled. She might not be Loretta Van Lochen anymore, her books might not be published, but she had Miles, and that was the important thing. She would never stop writing, even if no one read the stories except herself.

Some packets were already on the desk, and Miles opened one up. "Good. The butler must have brought this in."

"Something important?"

"It's for you," he said.

She blinked. "I just arrived here."

He handed her the packet. "Read the first page."

"A novel by Mary Jane Bolton." She gazed up at him. The man's beam was pleasant to see, but in this case, she couldn't understand the reason for his joy. "What does this have to do with me?"

"I hope you won't mind, sweetheart," Miles said, "but I know how important publishing your stories was to you."

"I can give that up," she said hastily. She didn't want the man to think her sad with her chosen life.

"I understand," Miles said, "because I also liked writing. I don't want to have an editor or publisher force me to write stories which hold no interest to me."

"Such as stories about penny dreadful novelists?" Veronique raised an eyebrow, and Miles flushed.

"I'm so sorry sweetheart for what I said." He clasped hold of her hands. "I was wrong to speak dismissively of them. Writing about women, showing them to expect the best in themselves and others—it is admirable."

"Good."

"That's why I thought we could start our own publishing company."

Veronique blinked.

"I know it might sound mad, but some people are doing it. I have the capital. A friend in New York is interested in working with us on the project. He's a businessman and is very enthusiastic about the idea. I thought I could oversee non-fiction books and you can oversee the fiction books. Would you like that?"

"T-that would be wonderful."

She wouldn't have to stop sharing her stories with others. She would even be able to work with new authors, people like herself, and help them connect with readers.

Miles smiled. "And of course you can decide how much writing and how much business you would like to do. I think I would like to write a non-fiction book. Perhaps we might visit Italy so I could research how life is there after the war?"

Italy.

She swung her arms around his neck. She was happy she'd tried to make her own path and that she'd never given up.

"I think you'll feel more comfortable there," Miles

continued. "The people are more friendly than in England."

"And I might blend in better?"

"You have too much spirit to ever blend in anywhere," Miles said. "And that's one of many, many, *many* reasons I love you."

"I love you too," she said solemnly.

"I know." Miles grinned and lifted her back into his arms.

Veronique's heart beat happily as Miles carried her in sturdy arms. The world tilted and swayed, but everything was wonderful.

"Now I think I should show you the rest of the manor house," Miles said. "Especially our bedroom. I might have to take a long time showing that to you."

Epilogue

"Scotland didn't seem so far away last time we visited," Veronique mused.

"That's because you were occupied with evading me," Miles said smugly. "A great intellectual challenge that would leave anyone quite incapable of assessing the passage of time with accuracy."

Veronique's face contorted into a frown, and in the next second she flung a pillow toward him.

The silk and tasseled concoction smacked his chest, and he held it gingerly in his hands. "How are you able to catch me off guard better than any of the talented men I used to play against with regularity at the club?"

She smiled, and he pulled her toward him. The coach was empty, save for them. No women in frilly dresses fluttered their eyelashes at him, and no stern-faced woman plotted to make him hers.

The curtains were pulled back, and light glowed from the outside. Sheep and goats directed their heads toward the carriage, perhaps astounded to see something besides their shepherd winding up the steep hills.

Miles had the vague sense he shouldn't be wondering at the fluffiness of the sheep's fur, and his lips shouldn't be moving into a smile at lambs leaping over the thick dark green blades that coated the Highlands. His heart shouldn't be moved by the mere sight of mammals grazing.

It was happiness.

He'd thought himself content before, flaunting the frequency of his placement in broadsheets to his brothers. If other people had told him with regularity that he should be happy, then he himself might have believed it. He hadn't known what happiness was before he met Veronique.

The coach tilted upward, a sign they were nearly at the castle. He almost felt irritated he would have to exit the carriage. How could anything be improved upon spending time with his wife?

Sunlight splattered over the dark stone of the castle. Miles imagined the past workers who must have carved the stone from some nearby quarry and the mules who must have dragged it onto the top of the hill, where the castle might look most intimidating to any mischievous Vikings or Englishmen.

The sunlight didn't manage to soften the foreboding structure, but the appearance of his older brother and blonde-haired sister-in-law, were more effective.

"Miles!" His brother's voice boomed, and he rushed toward the carriage. Somehow the burliness of his figure did not affect the speed of his strides, and in the next moment the man flung the carriage door open. His dark eyes sparkled.

"Gerard," Miles said.

Gerard poked his head into the carriage. "Lady Worthing. It's a pleasure to see you again."

Veronique nodded.

"You gave us a horrible scare last time," Gerard said.

"No fear of heights," Miles said fondly. He took his wife's hand and led her down the steps toward the castle.

"So if climbing down castle walls is your instinct when facing a possible marriage to this man, what is life with him really like?" Gerard asked. "Tell me if he's spending too much time in London. The man's too fond of clubs."

Veronique laughed. "My husband is far too fond of his home to leave."

"Oh?" Gerard's eyebrows rose, but Miles nodded.

Warmth tinged his cheeks, but he held his gaze firm. It was all true.

The sparkle in his brother's eyes softened. "Come, let's walk down to the chapel."

Miles offered his arm to Veronique, and they followed his brother. It was all too easy to remember the last time they'd ambled over the path. Each step had seemed painful, pulling him closer to the castle and an impending marriage with Veronique.

How little had he known then.

The only thing that might possibly bring him sorrow now was the thought that he might not continue to spend the rest of his life with her.

Gerard pushed open the doors of the chapel. For a brief moment they were once again swathed in darkness, but merry voices and the tinkling of a baby babbling sounded from inside.

Miles followed his brother into the chapel. This time when the door opened he was not confronted by the image of Veronique, clothed in a flowing wedding dress: they were already married, and she was at his side.

His sister-in-law smiled and strode toward him,

clutching a blanket to her in which he could only assume was his nephew. "You're here. We thought you would miss it."

"Never," Miles said.

"May I present you to your nephew, the future Marquess of Highgate?" Lady Rockport's words may have been formal, but her tone was far warmer than anything that should have befit a woman once crowned as the ton's ice queen.

His sister-in-law turned, and he glanced at the tiny figure gurgling happily in her arms.

"A pleasure." Miles bowed and reached to grasp his nephew's hand, noting the tininess of his fingers and fingernails.

Lady Rockport smiled. "I believe you've already met our local vicar."

Miles's back straightened.

"Ah, it's you." The vicar seemed to eye him warily, contorting his thin eyebrows.

"Indeed."

The vicar glanced behind him. "And—"

"Lady Worthing," Miles said shortly.

"Ah—so I heard," the vicar said. The skepticism in the man's voice did not precisely change. "I would have married you here. No need to have cavorted all the way to—" the man's eyes widened, and his voice lowered, as if fearful of disturbing the baby, "—England."

Lady Rockport laughed. "Need I remind you that I am English as well?"

The vicar's face reddened. "Well, technically I suppose. Though I don't think you really count. What with your Scottish spirit and all. No one could ever suspect."

"Let's get on with it," Gerard said, rubbing his hands. "Enough torturing the English."

The vicar nodded. Miles led his wife into a pew, smiling at his other relatives who'd made the journey.

The chapel remained as magical as it had the first time he'd seen Veronique. Sunbeams ushered vibrant colors through the stained glass, and stone flowers crept up the Corinthian columns.

He wrapped his fingers about his wife's hand. Perhaps one day, perhaps even soon, they might be standing where his brother and sister-in-law stood. Perhaps they might be holding their own child.

Sentiment washed over him, carrying him with more swiftness than any horse ever had. He leaned toward Veronique. "Do you find it dreadful that I would not be aghast at having a child?"

She clamped her lips together as if to contain a laugh. "Not at all."

"Good." He glanced at his wife, more aware of the preciousness that surrounded him and how close he'd come to not having any of it.

The vicar began his sermon, rambling in solemn tones about the weightiness of the action today. Though Miles had expressed some skepticism at the prospect of attending the christening, he soon relaxed.

Veronique's eyes glimmered, and she pressed her hand against his. "I was always right to be mad about the baron."

89278640R00140

Made in the USA
Lexington, KY
25 May 2018